Praise for the Alcatraz Series

"This is an excellent choice to read aloud to the whole family. It's funny, exciting, and briskly paced."
—*NPR* on *Alcatraz vs. the Evil Librarians*

"Genuinely funny . . . Plenty here to enjoy."
—*Locus* on *Alcatraz vs. the Evil Librarians*

"Like Lemony Snicket and superhero comics rolled into one (and then revved up on steroids), this nutty novel . . . [is] also sure to win passionate fans."
—*Publishers Weekly* (starred review) on *Alcatraz vs. the Evil Librarians*

"The conventional trappings of the middle school fantasy get turned upside down in this zany novel. . . . Readers who prefer fantasy with plenty of humor should enjoy entering Alcatraz's strange but amusing world."
—*School Library Journal* on *Alcatraz vs. the Evil Librarians*

"In this original, hysterical homage to fantasy literature, Sanderson's first novel for youth recalls the best in Artemis Fowl and A Series of Unfortunate Events. The humor, although broad enough to engage preteens, is also sneakily aimed at adults. . . . And as soon as they finish the last wickedly clever page, they will be standing in line for more from this seasoned author."
—*VOYA* on *Alcatraz vs. the Evil Librarians*

"A thoroughly thrilling read."

—*The Horn Book* on *The Scrivener's Bones*

"Those who enjoy their fantasy with a healthy dose of slapstick humor will be delighted. Give this novel to fans of Eoin Colfer's Artemis Fowl and Catherine Jinks's Cadel Piggott in *Evil Genius*. They will appreciate Sanderson's cheerful sarcastic wit and none-too-subtle digs at librarians."

—*School Library Journal* on *The Scrivener's Bones*

"Every bit as clever, fast-paced, and original as [the first book] . . . Howlingly funny for adults, older teens who can be persuaded to read a 'juvenile' novel, and exceptionally bright middle schoolers."

—*VOYA* on *The Scrivener's Bones*

"With comical insight into human nature and just enough substance to make it all matter, the plot offers up plenty of action, gadgetry, metafictional humor, grudgingly dispensed hints of the Librarians' endgame, and counterintuitive Smedry Talents to keep the old fans and new readers alike turning pages."

—*The Horn Book* on *The Knights of Crystallia*

"Offbeat humor, a budding romance, plenty of magic, creative world-building, smart references to science fiction luminaries, clever wordplay, and good action scenes make this one a strong choice for young teen boys and adult fans of the SF genre. . . . Hard to imagine it being any better written."

—*VOYA* on *The Knights of Crystallia*

"Lives up to its predecessors with vivid action and high drama."
                    —*Midwest Book Review* on *The Knights of Crystallia*

"Beneath the wild humor, there are surprisingly subtle messages about responsibility and courage."
                    —*School Library Journal* on *The Knights of Crystallia*

"As goofy randomness streamlines into compelling narration, even readers who don't find giant robots reason alone to pick up a book will be drawn into Alcatraz's cohesive world, with its unique form of magic." —*The Horn Book* on *The Shattered Lens*

"I love this series! Sanderson's one of the few writers of adult fiction I've read who can also write effortlessly and dead-on true for kids as well. This is a fabulous book to read aloud! It's not only funny and has plenty of action, but the series has got heart as well. Highly recommended!"
                    —*YA Books Central* on *The Shattered Lens*

BY BRANDON SANDERSON

ALCATRAZ VS. THE EVIL LIBRARIANS

Alcatraz vs. the Evil Librarians
The Scrivener's Bones
The Knights of Crystallia
The Shattered Lens
The Dark Talent (forthcoming)

The Rithmatist

THE MISTBORN TRILOGY

Mistborn
The Well of Ascension
The Hero of Ages

THE RECKONERS

Steelheart
Firefight
Calamity

THE
SHATTERED
LENS

BRANDON SANDERSON

Illustrations by
HAYLEY LAZO

A Tom Doherty Associates Book * New York

THE SHATTERED LENS

Copyright © 2010 by Dragonsteel Entertainment, LLC

Illustrations copyright © 2016 by Dragonsteel Entertainment, LLC

Reading and Activity Guide copyright © 2016 by Tor Books

Brandon Sanderson ® is a registered trademark of Dragonsteel Entertainment, LLC.

All rights reserved.

Illustrations by Hayley Lazo

Map by Isaac Stewart

A Starscape Book
Published by Tom Doherty Associates, LLC
175 Fifth Avenue
New York, NY 10010

www.tor-forge.com

The Library of Congress Cataloging-in-Publication Data is available upon request.

ISBN 978-0-7653-7900-9 (hardcover)
ISBN 978-1-4668-6556-3 (e-book)

Our books may be purchased in bulk for promotional, educational, or business use. Please contact your local bookseller or the Macmillan Corporate and Premium Sales Department at 1-800-221-7945, extension 5442, or by e-mail at MacmillanSpecialMarkets@macmillan.com.

First published in the United States by Scholastic Press, an imprint of Scholastic Inc.

First Starscape Edition: July 2016

Printed in the United States of America

0 9 8 7 6 5 4

For Peter Ahlstrom
Who is not only a good friend and great man,
But one who has been reading my books since the days
when they were terrible,
And who strives very hard to keep them from being
that way again.
Insoluble, Incalculable, Indefinable.
Indispensable.

ALCATRAZ VS. THE EVIL LIBRARIANS

THE SHATTERED LENS

Author's Foreword

I am an idiot.

You should know this already, if you've read the previous three volumes of my autobiography. If by chance you haven't read them, then don't worry. You'll get the idea. After all, nothing in this book will make any kind of sense to you. You'll be confused at the difference between the Free Kingdoms and the Hushlands. You'll wonder why I keep pretending that my glasses are magical. You'll be baffled by all these insane characters.

(Actually, you'll probably wonder all of those same things if you start from the beginning too. These books don't really make a lot of sense, you see. Try living through one of them sometime. Then you'll know what it really means to be confused.)

Anyway, as I was saying, if you haven't read the other three books, then don't bother. That will make this book even more confusing to you, and that's exactly what I want. By way of introduction, just let me say this: My name is Alcatraz Smedry, my Talent is breaking things, and I'm stoopid. Really, really stoopid. So stoopid, I don't know how to spell the word stupid.

This is my story. Or, well, part four of it. Otherwise known as "The part where everything goes wrong, and then Alcatraz has a cheese sandwich."

Enjoy.

Chapter 2

So there I was, holding a pink teddy bear in my hand. It had a red bow and an inviting, cute, bearlike smile. Also, it was ticking.

"Now what?" I asked.

"Now you throw it, idiot!" Bastille said urgently.

I frowned, then tossed the bear to the side, through the open window, into the small room filled with sand. A second later, an explosion blasted back through the window and threw me into the air. I was propelled backward, then slammed into the far wall.

With an "urk" of pain, I slid down and fell onto my back. I blinked, my vision fuzzy. Little flakes of plaster—the kind they put on ceilings just so they can break off and fall to the ground dramatically in an explosion—broke off the ceiling and fell dramatically to the ground. One hit me on the fore-head.

"Ow," I said. I lay there, staring upward, breathing in and out. "Bastille, did that teddy bear just explode?"

"Yes," she said, walking over and looking down at me. She had on a gray-blue militaristic uniform, and wore her straight, silver hair long. On her belt was a small sheath that had a large hilt sticking out of it. That hid her Crystin blade; though the sheath was only about a foot long, if she drew the weapon out it would be the length of a regular sword.

"Okay. Right. *Why* did that teddy bear just explode?"

"Because you pulled out the pin, stupid. What else did you expect it to do?"

I groaned, sitting up. The room around us—inside the Nalhallan Royal Weapons Testing Facility—was white and featureless. The wall where we'd been standing had an open window looking into the blast range, which was filled with sand. There were no other windows or furniture, save for a set of cabinets on our right.

"What did I expect it to do?" I said. "Maybe play some music? Say 'mama'? Where I come from, exploding is not a normal bear habit."

"Where you come from, a lot of things are backward," Bastille said. "I'll bet your poodles don't explode either."

"No, they don't."

"Pity."

"Actually, exploding poodles *would* be awesome. But exploding teddy bears? That's dangerous!"

"Duh."

"But Bastille, they're for *children*!"

"Exactly. So that they can defend themselves, obviously." She rolled her eyes and walked back over to the window that looked into the sand-filled room. She didn't ask if I was hurt. She could see that I was still breathing, and that was generally good enough for her.

Also, you may have noticed that this is Chapter Two. You may be wondering where Chapter One went. It turns out that I—being stoopid—lost it. Don't worry, it was kind of boring anyway. Well, except for the talking llamas.

I climbed to my feet. "In case you were wondering—"

"I wasn't."

"—I'm fine."

"Great."

I frowned, walking up to Bastille. "Is something bothering you, Bastille?"

"Other than you?"

"I *always* bother you," I said. "And you're always a little grouchy. But today you've been downright *mean*."

She glanced at me, arms folded. Then I saw her expression soften faintly. "Yeah."

I raised an eyebrow.

"I just don't like losing."

"Losing?" I said. "Bastille, you recovered your place in the knights, exposed and defeated a traitor to your order, and stopped the Librarians from kidnapping or killing the Council of Kings. If that's 'losing,' you've got a really funny definition of the word."

"Funnier than your face?"

"Bastille," I said firmly.

She sighed, leaning down, crossing her arms on the windowsill. "She Who Cannot Be Named got away, your mother escaped with an irreplaceable book in the Forgotten Language, and—now that they're not hiding behind the ruse of a treaty—the Librarians are throwing everything they've got at Mokia."

"You've done what you could. *I've* done what I could. It's time to let others handle things."

She didn't look happy about that. "Fine. Let's get back to your explosives training." She wanted me well prepared in case the war came to Nalhalla. It wasn't likely to happen, but my ignorance of proper things—like exploding teddy bears—has always been a point of frustration to Bastille.

Now, I realize that many of you are just as ignorant as I

am. That's why I prepared a handy guide that explains everything you need to know and remember about my autobiography in order to not be confused by this book. I put the guide in Chapter One. If you ever have trouble, you can reference it. I'm such a nice guy. Dumb, but nice.

Bastille opened one of the cabinets on the side wall and pulled out another small, pink teddy bear. She handed it to me as I walked up to her. It had a little tag on the side that said "Pull me!" in adorable lettering.

I took it nervously. "Tell me honestly. Why do you build grenades that look like teddy bears? It's not about protecting children."

"Well, how do you feel when you look at that?"

I shrugged. "It's cute. In a deadly, destructive way." *Kind of like Bastille,* I thought. "It makes me want to smile. Then it makes me want to run away screaming, since I know it's really *a grenade.*"

"Exactly," Bastille said, taking the bear from me and pulling the tag—the pin—out. She tossed it through the window. "If you build weapons that *look* like weapons, then everyone will know to run away from them! This way, the Librarians are confused."

"That's sick," I said. "Shouldn't I be ducking or something?"

"You'll be fine," she said.

Ah, I thought. *This one must be some kind of dud or fake.*

At that second, the grenade outside the window exploded. Another blast threw me backward. I hit the wall with a grunt, and another piece of plaster fell on my head. This time though, I managed to land on my knees.

Oddly, I felt remarkably unharmed, considering I'd just been blown backward by the explosion. In fact, neither explosion seemed to have hurt me very badly at all.

"The pink ones," Bastille said, "are blast-wave grenades. They throw people and things away from them, but they don't actually hurt anyone."

"Really?" I said, walking up to her. "How does *that* work?"

"Do I look like an explosives expert?"

I hesitated. With those fiery eyes and that dangerous expression . . .

"The answer is no, Smedry," she said flatly, folding her arms. "I don't know how these things work. I'm just a soldier."

She picked up a blue teddy bear and pulled the tag off, then tossed it out the window. I braced myself, grabbing the windowsill, preparing for a blast. This time, however, the bear grenade made a muted thumping sound. The sand in the next room began to pile up in a strange way, and I was suddenly yanked *through* the window into the next room.

I yelped, tumbling through the air, then hit the mound of sand face-first.

"That," Bastille said from behind, "is a *suction-wave* grenade. It explodes in reverse, pulling everything toward it instead of pushing it away."

"Mur murr mur mur murrr," I said, since my head was buried in the sand. Sand, it should be noted, does *not* taste very good. Even with ketchup.

I pulled my head free and leaned against the pile of sand, straightening my Oculator's Lenses and looking back at the window, where Bastille was leaning with arms crossed, smiling faintly. There's nothing like seeing a Smedry get sucked through a window to improve her mood.

"That should be impossible!" I protested. "A grenade that explodes *backward*?"

She rolled her eyes again. "You've been in Nalhalla for months now, Smedry. Isn't it time to stop pretending that everything shocks or confuses you?"

"I . . . er . . ." I wasn't pretending. I'd been raised in the Hushlands, trained by Librarians to reject things that seemed too . . . well, too strange. But Nalhalla—city of castles—was nothing *but* strangeness. It was hard not to get overwhelmed by it all.

"I still think a grenade shouldn't be able to explode *inward*," I said, shaking sand off my clothing as I walked up to the window. "I mean, how would you even make that work?"

"Maybe you take the same stuff you put in a regular grenade, then put it in backward?"

"I . . . don't think it works that way, Bastille."

She shrugged, getting out another bear. This one was purple. She moved to pull the tag.

"Wait!" I said, scrambling through the window. I took the bear grenade from her. "This time you're going to tell me what it does first."

"That's no fun."

I raised a skeptical eyebrow at her.

"This one is harmless," she said. "A stuff-eater grenade. It vaporizes everything nearby that *isn't* alive. Rocks, dead wood, fibers, glass, metal. All gone. But living plants, animals, people—perfectly safe. Works wonders against Alivened."

I looked down at the little purple bear. Alivened were objects brought to life through Dark Oculary. I'd once fought some created from romance novels. "This could be useful."

"Yeah," she said. "Works well against Librarians too. If a group is charging at you with those guns of theirs, you can vaporize the weapons but leave the Librarians unharmed."

"And their clothing?" I asked.

"Gone."

I hefted the bear, contemplating a little payback for being sucked through the window. "So you're saying that if I threw this at you, and it went off, you'd be left—"

"Kicking you in the face?" Bastille asked coolly. "Yes. Then I'd staple you to the outside of a tall castle and paint 'dragon food' over your head."

"Right," I said. "Er . . . why don't we just put this one away?"

"Yeah, good idea." She took it from me and stuffed it back into the cabinet.

"So . . . I noticed that none of those grenades are, well, *deadly.*"

"Of course they aren't," Bastille said. "What do you take us for? Barbarians?"

"Of course not. But you *are* at war."

"War's no excuse for *hurting* people."

I scratched my head. "I thought war was all *about* hurting people."

"That's Librarian thinking," Bastille said, folding her arms and narrowing her eyes. "Uncivilized." She hesitated. "Well, even the *Librarians* use many nonlethal weapons in war these days. You'll see, if the war ever comes here."

"All right . . . but you don't have any objections to hurting *me* on occasion."

"You're a Smedry," she said. "That's different. Now do you want to learn the rest of these grenades or not?"

"That depends. What are they going to do to me?"

She eyed me, then grumbled something and turned away.

I blinked. I'd gotten used to Bastille's moods by now, but this seemed irregular even for her. "Bastille?"

She walked over to the far side of the room, tapping a section of glass, making the wall turn translucent. The Royal Weapons Testing Facility was a tall, multitowered castle on the far side of Nalhalla City. Our vantage point gave us a great view of the capital.

"Bastille?" I asked again, walking up to her.

She said, arms folded, "I shouldn't be berating you like this."

"How *should* you be berating me, then?"

"Not at all. I'm sorry, Alcatraz."

I blinked. An apology. From *Bastille*? "The war really is bothering you, isn't it? Mokia?"

"Yeah. I just wish there were more to do. More that *we* could do."

I nodded, understanding. My escape from the Hushlands had snowballed into the rescue of my father from the Library of Alexandria, and following that we'd gotten sucked into stopping Nalhalla from signing a treaty with the Librarians. Now, finally, things had settled down. And not surprisingly, other people—people with more experience than Bastille and I—had taken over doing the most important tasks. I was a Smedry and she a full Knight of Crystallia, but we were both only thirteen. Even in the Free Kingdoms—where people didn't pay as much attention to age—that meant something.

Bastille had been rushed through training during her childhood and had obtained knighthood at a very young age. The others of her order expected her to do a lot of practice and training to make up for earlier lapses. She spent half of every day seeing to her duties in Crystallia.

Generally, I spent my days in Nalhalla learning. Fortunately, this was a *whole* lot more interesting than school had been back home. I was trained in things like using Oculatory Lenses, conducting negotiations, and using Free Kingdomer weapons. Being a Smedry—I was coming to learn—was like being a mix of secret agent, special forces commando, diplomat, general, and cheese taster.

I won't lie. It was shatteringly cool. Instead of sitting around all day writing biology papers or listening to Mr. Layton from algebra class extol the virtues of complex factoring, I got to throw teddy bear grenades and jump off buildings. It was really fun at the start.

Okay, it was really fun the WHOLE TIME.

But there was something missing. Before, though I'd been

stumbling along without knowing what I was doing, we'd been involved in important events. Now we were just . . . well, kids. And that was annoying.

"Something needs to happen," I said. "Something exciting." We looked out the window expectantly.

A bluebird flew by. It didn't, however, explode. Nor did it turn out to be a secret Librarian ninja bird. In fact, despite my dramatic proclamation, nothing at all interesting happened. And nothing interesting will happen for the next three chapters.

Sorry. I'm afraid this is going to be a rather boring book. Take a deep breath. The worst part is coming next.

Chapter

6

hew! Those were some *boring* chapters, weren't they? I know you really didn't want to hear—in intricate detail—about the workings of the Nalhallan sewer systems. Nor did you care to get a scholarly explanation of the original Nalhallan alphabet and how the letters are based on logographic representations of ancient Cabafloo. And, of course, that vibrant, excruciatingly specific description of what it's like to get your stomach pumped probably made you feel sick.

Don't worry though. These scenes are extremely important to Chapter Thirty-Seven of the novel. Without Chapters Three, Four, and Five, you would be *completely* lost when we get to a later point in the book. It's for your own good that I included them. You'll thank me later.

"Wait," I said, pointing out through the clear glass wall of the grenade testing room. "I recognize that bird."

Not the bluebird. The giant glass bird rising from the city a short distance away. It was called *Hawkwind*, and it had carried me on my first trip to Nalhalla. It was about the size of a small airplane and was constructed completely of beautiful translucent glass.

Now, some of you Hushlanders might wonder how I could recognize that particular vessel among all of those that were flying in and out of Nalhalla. That's because in the Hushlands, the Librarians make sure all vehicles look the same. All airplanes of a certain size look identical. Most cars pretty much look the same: trucks look like every other truck, sedans look like every other sedan. They let you change the color. Whoopee.

The Librarians claim it has to be this way, giving some gobbledygook about manufacturing costs or assembly lines. Those, of course, are lies. The real reason everything looks the same has to do with one simple concept: underpants.

I'll explain later.

The Free Kingdoms don't follow Hushlander ways of thinking. When they build something, they like to make it distinctive and original. Even an idiot like me could tell the difference between any two vehicles from a distance.

"*Hawkwind*," Bastille said, nodding as the glass bird

flapped its way into the sky, turning westward. "Isn't that the ship your father was outfitting for his secret mission?"

"Yes," I said.

"Do you think . . ."

"He just left without saying good-bye?" I watched *Hawkwind* streak away into the distance. "Yes."

* * *

"'To my father and son,'" Grandpa Smedry read, adjusting his Oculator's Lenses as he examined the note. "'I am bad at saying goodbye. Goodbye.'" He lowered the paper, shrugging.

"That's *it*?" Bastille exclaimed. "That's all he left?"

"Er, yes," Grandpa Smedry said, holding up two small orange pieces of paper. "That and what appears to be two coupons for half off a scoop of koala-flavored ice cream."

"That's terrible!" Bastille said.

"Actually, it's my favorite flavor," Grandpa replied, tucking the coupons away. "Quite considerate of him."

"I meant the note," she said, standing with arms folded. We had returned to Keep Smedry, an enormous black stone castle nestled on the far south side of Nalhalla City. Fireglass crackled on a hearth at the side of the room. Yes, in the Free Kingdoms there is a kind of glass that can burn. Don't ask.

"Ah yes," Grandpa said, rereading the note. "Yes, yes, yes.

You have to admit, though, he *is* very bad at good-byes. This note makes a very good argument for that. I mean, he even spelled good-bye wrong. Bad at it indeed!"

I sat in an overstuffed red chair beside the hearth. It was the chair on which we'd found the note. Apparently my father hadn't told anyone outside his inner circle that he was leaving. He'd gathered his group of soldiers, assistants, and explorers and then taken off.

We were the only three in the black-walled room. Bastille eyed me. "I'm sorry, Alcatraz," she said. "This has to be the *worst* thing he could have done to you."

"I don't know," Grandpa said. "The coupons could have been for Rocky Road instead." He cringed. "Dreadful stuff. Who puts a *road* in ice cream? I mean really."

Bastille regarded him evenly. "You're not helping."

"I wasn't really trying to," Grandpa said, scratching his head. He was bald save for a tuft of white hair running around the back of his head and sticking out behind his ears—like someone had stapled a cloud to his scalp—and he had a large white mustache. "But I suppose I should. Ragged Resnicks, lad! Don't look so glum. He's a horrible father anyway, right? At least he's gone now!"

"You're terrible at this," Bastille said.

"Ah, but *I* didn't spell anything wrong."

I smirked. I could see a twinkle in my grandfather's eyes.

He was just trying to cheer me up. He walked over, sitting down on the chair beside me. "Your father doesn't know what to make of you, lad. He didn't have a chance to grow into being a parent. I think he's scared of you."

Bastille sniffed in disdain. "So Alcatraz is just supposed to sit here in Nalhalla waiting for him to come back? Last time Attica Smedry vanished, it took him *thirteen years* to reappear. Who knows what he's even planning to do!"

"He's going after my mother," I said softly.

Bastille turned toward me, frowning.

"She has the book he wants," I said. "The one that has secrets on how to give everyone Smedry Talents."

"That's a specter your father has been chasing for many, many years, Alcatraz," Grandpa Smedry said. "Giving everyone Smedry Talents? I don't think it's possible."

"People said that about finding the Translator's Lenses too," Kaz noted. "But Attica managed that."

"True, true," Grandpa said. "But this is different."

"I guess," I said. "But—"

I froze, then turned to the side. My uncle, Kazan Smedry, sat in the third chair beside the fireplace. He was about four feet tall and, like most little people, hated being called a midget. He wore sunglasses, a brown leather jacket, and a tunic underneath that he tucked into a pair of rugged trousers. He was covered in black, sooty dust.

"Kaz!" I exclaimed. "You're back!"

"Finally!" he said, coughing.

"What . . ." I asked, indicating the soot.

"Got lost in the fireplace," Kaz said, shrugging. "Been in the blasted thing for a good two weeks now."

Every Smedry has a Talent. The Talent can be powerful, it can be unpredictable, and it can be disastrous. But it's always interesting. You could get one by being born a Smedry or by marrying a Smedry. My father wanted everyone to get a Talent.

And I was beginning to suspect that this was what my mother had been seeking all along. The Sands of Rashid, the years of searching, the theft from the Royal Archives (not a library) in Nalhalla—all of this was focused on finding a way to bestow Smedry Talents on people who didn't normally have them. I suspected that my father did it because he wanted to share our powers with everyone. I suspected that my mother, however, wanted to create an invincible, Talent-wielding Librarian army.

Now, I'm not too bright, but I figured that this was a bad thing. I mean, if Librarians had my Talent—breaking things? Here's a handy list of things I figure they'd probably break if they could:

Your lunch. Every day, when you'd open your lunch—no matter what you brought—you'd find it had been changed into a pickle-and-orange-slug sandwich. And there would be NO SALT.

Dance. You don't want to see any break dancing Librarians. Really. Trust me.

Recess. That's right. They'd break recess and turn it into a session of advanced algebra instead. (Note: The same thing happens when you go to middle school or junior high. Sorry.)

Wind. No explanation needed.

As you can see, it would be a disaster.

"Kazan!" Grandpa said, smiling toward his son.

"Hey, Pop."

"Still getting in trouble, I presume?"

"Always."

"Good lad. Trained you well!"

"Kaz," I said. "It's been months! What took you so long?"

Kaz grimaced. "The Talent."

In case you've forgotten, my grandfather had the Talent of arriving late to things, while Kaz had the Talent to get lost in rather amazing ways. (I don't know why I'm repeating this, since I clearly explained it all in Chapter One. Ah well.)

"Isn't that a long time to get lost, even for you?" Bastille asked, frowning.

"Yeah," Kaz said. "I haven't been *this* lost for years."

"Ah yes," Grandpa Smedry said. "Why, I remember your mother and I once spending upward of two months frantically searching for you when you were two, only to have you appear back in your crib one night!"

Kaz looked wistful. "I was an . . . interesting child to raise."

"All Smedrys are," Grandpa added.

"Oh?" Bastille said, finally sitting down in the fourth and final chair beside the hearth. "You mean there are Smedrys who eventually grow up? Can I get assigned to one of them sometime? It would be a nice change."

I chuckled, but Kaz just shook his head, looking distracted by something. "I've got my Talent under control again," he said. "Finally. But it took far too long. It's like . . . the Talent went haywire for a while. I haven't had to wrestle with it like this for years." He scratched his chin. "I'll have to write a *paper* about it."

Most members of my family, it should be noted, are some kind of professor, teacher, or researcher. It may seem odd to you that a bunch of dedicated miscreants like us are also a bunch of scholars. If you think that, it means you haven't known enough professors in your time. What better way is there to avoid growing up than to spend the rest of your life perpetually in school?

"Pelicans!" Kaz swore suddenly, standing up. "I don't have

time for a paper right now! I nearly forgot. Pop, while I was wandering around lost, I passed through Mokia. Tuki Tuki is besieged!"

"We know," Bastille said, her arms folded.

"We do?" Kaz said, scratching at his head.

"We've sent troops to help Mokia," Bastille said. "But the Librarians have begun to raid our nearby coasts. We can't give any more support to Mokia without leaving Nalhalla undefended."

"It's more than that, I'm afraid," Grandpa Smedry said. "There are . . . elements in the Council of Kings who are dragging their feet."

"What?" Kaz exclaimed.

"You missed the whole thing with the treaty, Son," Grandpa said. "I fear some of the monarchs have made alliances with the Librarians. They nearly got a motion through the Council to abandon Mokia entirely. That was defeated, but only by one vote. Those who were in favor of the motion are still working to deny support to Mokia. They have a lot of influence in the Council."

"But the Librarians tried to kill them!" I exclaimed. "What about the assassination attempt?"

As a side note, I hate assassination. It looks way too much like a dirty word. Either that or the name of a country populated entirely by two donkeys.

Grandpa just shrugged. "Bureaucrats, lad! They can be more dense than your uncle Kaz's bean soup."

"Hey!" Kaz said. "I like that soup!"

"I do too," Grandpa said. "Makes wonderful glue."

"We need to do something," Kaz said.

"I'm *trying* to," Grandpa said. "You should hear the speeches I'm giving!"

"Talk," Kaz said. "Tuki Tuki is close to falling, Pop! If the capital falls, the kingdom will fall with it."

"What about the Knights?" I said. "Bastille, didn't you say most of the Knights of Crystallia are still here in the city? Why aren't they on the battlefield?"

"The Crystin can't be used for that kind of purpose, lad," Grandpa said, shaking his head. "They're forbidden from taking sides in political conflicts."

"But this isn't a political conflict!" I said. "This is against the *Librarians*. They infiltrated the Crystin; they corrupted the Mindstone! If they win, they'll undoubtedly disband the knights anyway!"

Bastille grimaced. "You see why I'm on edge? We *know* all of this, but our oaths forbid us from taking part unless we're defending a Smedry or one of the monarchs."

"Well, one of the monarchs is in danger," I said. "Kaz just said so!"

"King Talakimallo isn't in the palace at Tuki Tuki," Grandpa said, shaking his head. "The knights got him away to a safe location soon after the palace came under siege. The queen is leading the defense."

"The queen of Mokia . . ." I said. "Bastille, isn't that . . ."

"My sister," she said, nodding. "Angola Dartmoor."

"The knights won't protect her?" I asked.

"She's not heir to a line," Bastille said, shaking her head. "They may have left one guard to protect her, but maybe not. The knights in the area probably all went with the king or with the heir, Princess Kamali."

"Tuki Tuki is a *hugely* important tactical position," Kaz said. "We can't lose it!"

"The knights *want* to help, but we can't," Bastille complained. "It's forbidden. Besides, most of us have to be here in Nalhalla City to defend the Council of Kings and the Smedrys."

"Though the Council no longer trusts the Crystin like they once did," Grandpa added, shaking his head. "And they forbid the knights entrance to most important meetings."

"So we just end up *sitting around*," Bastille said, frustratedly knocking her head against the back of her chair, "going through endless training sessions and throwing the occasional grenade at someone who deserves it." She eyed me.

"Baking Browns, what a mess!" Grandpa said. "Maybe we

need some snacks. I work better with a good broccoli yogurt pop to chew on."

"First," I said, "*ew*. Grandpa, that's almost crapaflapnasti. Second . . ." I hesitated for a moment, an idea occurring to me. "You're saying the knights have to protect important people."

Bastille gave me one of her trademarked "Well duh, Alcatraz, you idiot"™ looks. I ignored it.

"And the Mokian palace is besieged, about to fall?" I continued.

"That's what it looked like to me," Kaz said.

"So what if we sent someone really important off to Mokia?" I asked. "The knights would have to follow, right? And if we had that someone take up residence in the Mokian palace, then the knights would *have* to defend the place, right?"

At that moment, something incredible happened. Something amazing, something incredible, something unbelievable.

Bastille smiled.

It was a deep, knowing smile. An eager smile. Almost a *wicked* smile. Like the smile on a jack-o'-lantern carved by a psychopathic kitten. (Oh, wait. *All* kittens are psychopathic.

If you've forgotten, read book one again. In fact, read book one again either way. Someone told me once that it was really funny. What? You believed me in the prologue when I told you not to read them? What, you think you can trust *me*?)

Bastille's smile shocked me, pleased me, and made me nervous at the same time. "I think," she said, "that is just about the *most brilliant* thing you've ever said, Alcatraz."

Granted, the statement didn't have much competition for the title.

"It's certainly bold," Grandpa said. "Smedry-like for certain!"

"Who would we send?" Kaz said, growing eager. "Could you go, Pop? They'd be *certain* to send knights to defend you."

Grandpa hesitated, then shook his head. "If I did that, I'd leave Brig without an ally on the Council of Kings. He needs my vote."

"But we'd need a direct heir," Kaz said. "I could go—I *will* go—but I've never been important enough to warrant more than a single knight. I'm not the direct heir. We could send Attica."

"He's gone," Bastille said. "Fled the city. It's what we were talking about when you arrived."

Grandpa nodded. "We'd need to put someone in danger who is so valuable the knights *have* to respond. But this person also has to be *uncompromisingly* stoopid. It's idiocy on a grand scale to send oneself directly to a palace on the brink of destruction, surrounded by Librarians, in a doomed kingdom! Why, they'd have to be stoopid on a colossal degree. Of the likes previously unseen among all of humankind!"

And suddenly, for some reason, all eyes in the room turned toward me.

Chapter

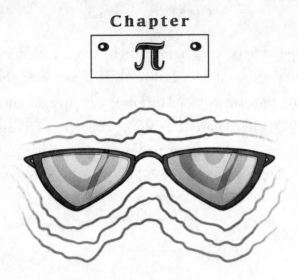

π

Okay, so maybe I exaggerated that last conversation just a little bit. Grandpa *might* have actually said something along the lines of "We'd need someone really, really brave." I felt that it's all right to make this swap, however, since bravery and stoopidity are practically one and the same.

There's a mathematical formula for it: STU ≥ BVE. That reads, quite simply, "A person's stoopidity is greater than or equal to their bravery." Simple, eh?

Oh, you want proof? You expect me to *justify* my ridiculous assertions? Well, all right. Just this once.

Look at it this way. If a man stumbled accidentally into a trap set by a group of Librarian agents, we'd think him stoopid. Right? However, if he charges valiantly into that same trap knowing it's there, he'd be called *brave*. Think about that for a moment. Which sounds dumber? Accidentally falling into the trap or *choosing* to fall into it?

There are plenty of ways to be stoopid that don't involve being brave. However, bravery is—by definition—always stoopid. Therefore, your stoopidity is *at least* equal to your level of bravery. Probably greater.

After all, reading that ridiculous explanation probably made you feel dumber just by association. (Reading this book sure is brave of you.)

I burst into the small meeting chamber. The monarchs sat in thrones arranged in a half circle, listening to one of their members—in this case, a woman in an ancient-looking suit of bamboo armor—stand before them and argue her point. The walls depicted murals of beautiful mountain scenes, and a little indoor stream gurgled its way along the far wall.

All of the monarchs turned toward me, eyes aghast at being interrupted.

"Ah, young Smedry!" said one of them, a regal-looking man with a square red beard and a set of kingly robes to match it. Brig Dartmoor, Bastille's father, was king of Nalhalla and generally considered foremost among the monarchs. He stood up from his chair. "How . . . unusual to see you."

The others looked panicked. I realized that the *last* time

I'd barged in on them like this, I'd come to warn them about a Librarian plot and had ended up nearly getting them all assassinated. (The non-donkey kind.)

I took a deep breath. "I can't take it any longer!" I exclaimed. "I hate being cooped up in this city! I need a vacation!"

The monarchs glanced at one another, relaxing slightly. I hadn't come to warn them of impending disaster; this was just the usual Smedry drama.

"Well, that's fine, I guess . . ." King Dartmoor said. Anyone else would probably have demanded to know why this "vacation" was so important as to interrupt the Council of Kings. But Dartmoor was quite accustomed to handling Smedrys. I was only just beginning to understand what a reputation for oddness my family had—and this was compared with everyone around them, who lived in a city filled with castles, dragons that climbed on walls, grenades that looked like teddy bears, and the occasional talking dinosaur in a vest. Being odd compared with all of them took *quite* a bit of effort. (My family is a bunch of overachievers when it comes to freakish behavior.)

"Perhaps you'd like to visit the countryside," said one of the kings. "The firelizard trees are in bloom."

"I hear the lightning caverns are electrifying this time of year," another added.

"You could go always try skydiving off the Worldspire," said the woman in the Asian-style bamboo armor. "Drop through the Bottomless Chasm for a few hours? It's rather relaxing, with a waterfall on all sides, falling through the air."

"Wow," I said, losing a bit of my momentum. "Those *do* sound interesting. Maybe I—" Bastille elbowed me from behind at that point, making me exclaim a surprised "Gak!"

"Protect your straw!" one of the monarchs cried, taking off his large straw hat. He looked around urgently. "Oh, false alarm."

I cleared my throat, glancing over my shoulder. Bastille and Grandpa Smedry had entered the room after me but had left the door open so that the knights guarding outside could hear what I was saying. Bastille's stern mother, Draulin, stood with folded arms, eyeing us suspiciously. She obviously expected some kind of shenanigan.

Very clever of her.

"No!" I declared to the monarchs. "None of that will do. They're not exciting enough." I held up my finger. "I'm going to Tuki Tuki. I hear that the royal mud baths there are *extremely* intense."

"Wait," King Dartmoor said. "You think *skydiving* through a *bottomless pit* in the ocean isn't exciting enough, so instead you want to go visit the Mokian palace spa?"

"Er, yes," I said. "I have a fondness for mud baths. Exfoliating my homeopathic algotherapy and all that."

The monarchs glanced at one another.

"But," one of them said, "the palace is *kind of* besieged right now, and—"

"I will not be dissuaded!" I exclaimed with forced bravado. "I am a Smedry, and we do ridiculous, unexpected, eccentric things like this all the time! Ha ha!"

"Oh dear," Grandpa Smedry said in an exaggerated voice. "He really does seem determined. My poor grandson will be killed because of his awesome, Smedry-like impulsiveness. If only there were a group of people dedicated to protecting him!"

With that, we turned and dashed away from the chamber, leaving the monarchs and knights standing dumbfounded. Bastille, Grandpa, and I entered the main palace hallway, which was lined with frames containing rare and exotic types of glass. They glowed faintly to my eyes, as I was still wearing my Oculator's Lenses.

"Do you think they'll buy it?" I asked.

"Wait," Bastille said, frowning. "Buy it? Did you try to sell them something?"

"Er, no. It's a figure of speech."

"The figure giving a speech?" Bastille said. "If you're *that* interested in her figure, you should be ashamed. Queen Kamiko is a married woman and *at least* forty years older than you are!"

I sighed. "Do you think," I rephrased, "they'll believe the act? It seemed a little exaggerated to me."

"Exaggerated?" Bastille said. "What part?"

"The part about me going to Mokia—into a war zone— just to take a vacation. It's kind of ridiculous."

"Sounds like a Smedry activity to me," Bastille grumbled.

"They'll buy it, lad," Grandpa said, jogging along beside us. "The knights in particular tend to be very . . . literal people. They'll assume the worst, and that worst—in this case—is that you are going to blunder off into a war zone because you feel that your pores are clogged. I don't think we'll have any trouble getting them to—"

A clanking sound came from behind us. I glanced over my shoulder.

No fewer than *fifty* Knights of Crystallia were rushing down the hallway in our direction.

"Gak!" I cried.

"Alcatraz, would you stop saying—" Bastille looked over her shoulder. "GAK!"

"Scribbling Scalzis!" Grandpa exclaimed, noticing the fleet of knights charging in our direction. Most wore full plate, the silvery metal clanking as their armored feet hit the floor. It sounded like someone had opened a closet filled with pots and then dumped them all onto the ground at once.

We redoubled our efforts, running in front of the storm of knights with all we had. But they were faster. They had Warrior's Lenses, not to mention Crystin enhancements. They'd catch us for sure.

"Alcatraz, lad," Grandpa Smedry said in a confiding tone as we ran down the wide hallway. "I believe I may have discovered a slight flaw in your clever plan."

"You think?"

"I knew this would happen!" Bastille said from my other side. "I'm such an *idiot*. Alcatraz, if they can catch you before you leave, they can take you into protective care for your own good!"

"Protective care?" I asked.

"Usually involves a locked door," Grandpa said. "Padded cell. Bread and water. Oh, and a jail. Can't forget that."

"They'll throw us in *jail*?" I exclaimed.

"Hmm, yes," Grandpa Smedry said. "The knights are bodyguards, lad. They have the right to determine when someone under their charge is going to be put into too much danger. They only have power to do it while we're inside Nalhalla." He smiled. "They rarely invoke the privilege. We must *really* have them worried! Good job, lad! You should feel proud."

This is a very exciting scene, isn't it? You're not too tired are you? From all that exciting running?

Wait, you're *not running*? Why am I doing all the work? Don't you realize that you're supposed to be acting out these scenes as I describe them? Don't you know how to read books? I mean honestly, what are the Librarians teaching people these days?

Let me explain it to you. Everyone always talks about the magic of books being able to take you to other places, to let you see exotic worlds, to make you experience new and interesting things. Well, do you think words alone can do this? Of course not!

If you've ever thought that books are boring, it's because you don't know how to read them correctly. From now on, when you read a book, I want you to scream the words of the novel out loud while reading them, then do exactly what the characters are doing in the story.

Trust me, it will make books *way* more exciting. Even dictionaries. *Particularly* dictionaries. So go ahead and try it out with the next part of this book. If you do it right, you'll win the bonus prize.

"Come on!" I yelled, ducking into a side room. I figured that the knights would have trouble following us through smaller chambers, since there were so many of them. The room was filled with furniture, however, and I was forced to leap up on top of a couch and hurl myself behind it.

"What do we do?" Bastille asked, looking over her shoulder. The knights were rushing into the room behind us.

"I'm not sure!" I said, picking my nose.

We burst out of the room into a hallway, where I hopped up and down on one foot three times, then punched myself (softly) in the forehead. After that, we pranced down the hallway flapping our arms like chickens. Then we twirled around, smacking our brother if he happened to be near. Then we stuck our feet in our mouths before dumping pudding on our heads while singing "Hambo the Great" in Dutch.

Now see, didn't I *tell* you it would be more exciting this way? You should act out all books you read. (And by the way, the bonus prize is getting to smack your brother and blame it on me.)

"Why are we doing this?" Bastille cried.

"It's not really helping, is it?" I replied.

"I don't mean to be depressing," Grandpa noted, "but I do think they're gaining on us."

It was an understatement. They were *right* behind us. I yelped, bolting down a side hallway, Bastille easily keeping up. She had Warrior's Lenses on and could outrun Grandpa and me, but she hung back.

"Only one thing for me to do!" Grandpa Smedry said, raising a finger.

"What's that?" I asked.

"Switch sides!" he replied. And then he stopping running, letting the knights catch up to him. "Come on, let's get him!" Grandpa cried, pointing at me.

I froze, looking at him, shocked. Bastille tugged me forward and I stumbled into motion, running again. The knights didn't take Grandpa into protective care. One did pick him up and carry him, however, so he didn't slow them

down. In seconds we were being chased not only by an entire force of Knights of Crystallia, but my mustachioed grandfather as well.

"What's he doing?" I demanded.

"Burn him at the stake!" Grandfather yelled from just behind.

"Well," Bastille said, "he never *was* going to go with us. Remember? When we acted in front of the monarchs, his part was to claim that he didn't want you to go and couldn't stop you."

"Dice him up and feed him to the fishes!" Grandpa yelled, voice softer.

"Why did we decide that again?" I sputtered.

"Pull his insides out through his nose and paint him with eyeliner!" Grandpa Smedry yelled distantly.

"Because we didn't want him to get into trouble for what you're doing!" Bastille said.

"Make him watch old *Little House on the Prairie* reruns!" Grandpa Smedry bellowed, voice dwindling.

"Well does he have to get into the part so enthusiastically?" I said. "He's making me . . . Wait, *voice dwindling*?" I glanced over my shoulder.

The knights and my grandfather had fallen back. I frowned, confused. The knights seemed to be running as hard as ever. In fact, they seemed to be running even *harder* than before. And yet they were still losing ground.

"What?" I said.

"He's making them late!" Bastille said. "Using his Talent! By joining their side, then trying to chase after us, he's making them all too slow to catch us!"

I gawked, amazed. My grandfather's skill with using his Talent was incredible. I wondered, not for the first time, what I could manage with my *own* Talent if I were as trained as he was. These last few months in Nalhalla, I'd mostly spent my time learning to *avoid* using my Talent. I had it almost completely under control. I hadn't broken anything unexpected in weeks.

I was beginning to think that I might be able to live a normal life. But sometimes when my grandfather did incredible things with his Talent, it made me envious.

That was stoopid. (And trust me, I'm an expert on stoopid.) I'd spent my entire childhood ruled and dominated by my Talent. Accomplishing something like Grandpa just did was incredible, but also unpredictable. Even the best of Smedrys couldn't make events like this work all the time.

I wanted to be rid of my Talent. Free. Didn't I?

"Gee, what a nice moment of reflection," Bastille said, stepping up to me.

"Yeah," I said, watching the troop of frustrated knights, who seemed to be all but running in place, barely inching forward.

"Do you want another moment or two to, you know, be all philosophical and crud? Or do you want to get your *shattering* legs moving so we can escape!"

"Oh, right," I said. Grandpa wouldn't be able to hold them back forever. In fact, they already looked like they were moving more quickly, regaining some momentum.

I turned with Bastille and continued running. We needed to get out of the city, and *fast*.

Chapter

It's undoubtedly becoming obvious to you that my stoopidity in this book is pretty shatteringly spectacular. Not only was I planning to charge off into a war zone with nothing to protect me but a couple of bits of glass, but I had managed to alienate and anger an entire order of knights in the process. I just spent the three previous volumes of my autobiography trying to *escape* the Librarians. Now that I had finally found peace and safety in Nalhalla, I'd decided to run off and put myself into the middle of the war?

Stoopid.

Actually, no, it's *not* stoopid. *Stoopid* just isn't specific enough. Fortunately, since I'm an expert on stoopidity—and an expert on making up stuff—I'm going to give you a set of *new* definitions to use for things that are really stoopid.

For example, what I was about to go do can be referred to as *stoopidalicious*, which is defined as "about as stoopid as a porcupine-catching contest during a swimsuit competition."

Bastille and I dashed up a set of stairs onto the upper level of the palace. Once there, I slammed a hand down on the top step and engaged my Talent. A shock of power ran down my arm, hitting the stairs and making them crumble away behind us. Stone blocks crashed to the ground and the banister fell sideways. An enormous puff of dust erupted into the air, like the noxious breath of a belching giant. As it cleared, I could see a group of annoyed knights standing below. They'd finally gotten smart and broken into two groups. Grandpa Smedry could keep only one group late, so the other group was free to chase Bastille and me.

Now they were trapped below. But there were other ways up to our floor. "I don't think we can keep staying ahead of them like this," I said. "We need to get out of the palace."

"You just said that at the end of the last chapter!" Bastille complained.

"Well it's still true!" I snapped. Below, the knights split again, some running off to find another way up. A few remained behind and began giving one another leg-ups or jumping. They got surprisingly close to reaching the upper floor.

I yelped and hurried away from the hole, Bastille following.

"Sorry about the stairs," I said. "Your father won't be mad at me for that, will he?"

"We have Smedrys over to the palace for dinner frequently," she said. "Things like broken staircases are routine for us. However, I *will* point out that you just trapped us on the upper floor of the palace. I'll bet my mother and the other knights will have the stairwells all blocked off shortly."

"Do you have a Transporter's Glass station?"

"Yeah. In the basement."

"It's guarded anyway," Kaz added.

I cursed. "You've got to have some kind of secret exit from the building, right, Bastille? Tunnels? Passages hidden in the walls? A fireplace that rotates around and reveals your secret crime-fighting lair?"

"Nope," Kaz said.

Bastille nodded. "My father feels that sort of thing is too easy for enemies to use against him."

"No secret passages at all?" I exclaimed. "What kind of castle *is* this?"

"The non-stoopidalicious kind!" Bastille said. "Who puts passages *inside* the walls? Isn't that a little ridiculous?"

"Not when you need to sneak out!"

"Why would I need to sneak out of my own home?"

"Because Knights of Crystallia are chasing you!"

"This sort of thing doesn't happen to me very often!" Bastille snapped. "In fact, it *only* seems to happen when you're involved!"

"I can't help the fact that people like to chase me. We need to—"

I froze in the middle of the hallway. "Kaz!" I exclaimed, pointing at him.

"Me!" he exclaimed back.

"Idiots!" Bastille said, pointing at both of us.

"When did you get here?" I demanded of my short uncle.

"A few moments ago," he said. "Everything's packed at Keep Smedry, ready for takeoff. I borrowed a vehicle from the Mokian embassy, as I didn't want to alert the king of what we were doing."

"We have a pilot?" I asked.

"Sure do," he replied. "Aydee Ecks."

"Who?"

"Your cousin," he said. "Sister to Sing and Australia. She was delivering a message to the embassy from Mokia."

"Sounds good," I said. It was always nice to have another Smedry along on a mission. Well, nice and catastrophic at the same time. But when you're a Smedry, you learn to make the catastrophes work for you.

A distant clanking preceded a group of knights, who stormed out of a side hallway a moment later. They spotted us and began running in our direction.

"Kaz!" I said. "Get us out of here!"

"Are you sure?" he said. "My Talent has been—"

"Now, Kaz!" I said.

"All right," he said with a sigh, walking over and pulling open a door. We'd used Kaz's Talent of getting lost to transport us before. Like all Smedry Talents, it was unpredictable— but it was fairly safe to use across short distances.

Besides, we didn't have time to try anything else. I ran through the doorway, Bastille behind me. Kaz followed and pulled the door closed.

The room smelled musty and wet inside, like mold or fungus, but it was too dark to see anything.

"Activate your Talent!" I told Kaz.

"I already did," he replied.

There was a scraping noise. Like something very large being pulled across the stone floor. I blinked as Bastille unsheathed her sword, the crystalline weapon shedding a cool blue light across our surroundings. We were in a cave. And standing before us, looking very confused, was an enormous black dragon. It cocked its head at us, smoke trailing from its nostrils.

"Well," I said, relieved. "It's just a dragon. For a moment, I

was frightened!" We'd met a dragon before, and it had quite nicely *not* eaten us. In fact, it had carried us on its back.

The dragon inhaled deeply.

"Kaz!" Bastille said, panicked.

"Put away that light!" he said. "It's hard to get lost if I can see where I'm going!"

I frowned at the others. "It's just a dragon."

"Just a free baledragon," Bastille said with alarm, "who—unlike Tzoctinatin—is not serving a prison sentence, and who is perfectly justified in roasting us because we're invading his den and violating the draco-human treaty!" She slammed her sword back in its sheath, plunging us into darkness.

"Oh," I said.

A light appeared in front of us, illuminating the inside of the dragon's mouth as fire gathered in its throat and began to blast toward us.

"Reason number two hundred and fifty-seven why it's better to be a short person than a tall person!" Kaz exclaimed. "Standing next to a tall person gives you a really great shield for dragon's breath!"

Bastille grabbed me by the collar and yanked me hard after her, and everything spun. I felt a strange *force* around me, a lurching feeling as Kaz activated his Talent, getting us lost. The dragon's flames vanished.

I recognized that force—the force of the Talent—immediately, though I'd never experienced it before when Kaz had used his Talent. It was hard to explain. It felt like I could see the warping of the air, could tell what was going on as Kaz saved us.

It almost seemed familiar. Like Kaz wasn't just getting us lost, like he was . . . well, like he was *breaking* the way that motion worked. Deconstructing the natural, linear progression of the world and rebuilding it so that we could move in directions we shouldn't have been able to.

In that moment, I thought I saw something. An enormous, magnificent stone disc, full of carvings and etchings, divided into four different quadrants. And at the very center, a patch of black rock. There was something crouching there in the center, invisible because of how dark it was. A patch of midnight itself. And it reached tentacles out to the other quadrants, like black vines growing over a wall.

The Bane of Incarna. That which twists . . . that which corrupts . . . that which destroys . . .

The Dark Talent. Of which all others are shadows.

The vision vanished, gone so quickly that I wasn't certain I'd even seen it. Everything was dark again, and I stumbled, tripping. When I hit the ground, I hit something wet, soft, and squishy.

"Ew!" I said, trying to push myself to my feet. The floor

undulated beneath me, pulsing, quivering. It was like I'd fallen onto a massive trampoline covered with slick grease. And the stench was *terrible*. Like someone had pelted a skunk with rotten eggs.

Bastille made a gagging nose, pulling her sword from its sheath to give us light. The three of us were crowded together inside a pink room, the walls and ceiling all made of the same soft, quivering material. It was like we were trapped in some kind of sack. There wasn't room enough to sit up, and we were coated with a slick, gooey substance.

"Aw, sparrows," Kaz swore.

"I think I'm going to be sick!" Bastille said. "Are we . . . ?"

"My Talent transported us into the dragon's stomach, it appears," Kaz said, scratching his head, trying to stand up on the fleshy surface. "Whoops."

"Whoops?" I cried, realizing that the liquidy stuff had to be some kind of bile or phlegm. "That's all you can say? Whoops?"

"Ew!" Bastille said.

"Well, if we're going to be eaten by a dragon," he noted, "this is the way to do it. Bypassing the teeth and such."

"I'd rather not be eaten at all!"

"Ew!" Bastille repeated.

"Hide the sword," Kaz said, finally getting to his feet. He was short enough to stand upright. "I'll get us out of here."

"Great," I said, the light winking out. "Maybe you could get us a bath too, and—gruble-garb-burgle!"

I was suddenly underwater.

I thrashed about in the dark, terrified, suffocating. The water was horribly cold, and my skin grew numb in a few heartbeats. I opened my mouth to cry out—

Which, mind you, was a pretty stoopidalicious thing to do.

And then I washed out into open air, water rushing around me as I fell through an open doorway. Kaz stood to the side, gasping, holding the door open. He'd managed to get us to Keep Smedry; a familiar black stone hallway led in either direction.

I sat up, holding my head, my clothing wet. We appeared to have fallen out of the cleaning closet, and the floor of the hallway was now soaked with salty seawater. A few small, white-eyed fish flopped around on the stones. Bastille lay in front of me, her hair a soggy silver mass. She groaned and sat up, flipping her hair back.

"Where were we?" I asked.

"Bottom of the ocean," Kaz said, taking off his soaked leather jacket and eyeing it appraisingly.

"The pressure should have killed us!"

"Nah," Kaz said, wringing out his jacket, "we surprised her. We were gone before she realized we were there."

"Her?" I asked.

"The ocean," Kaz said. "She never expects Smedry Talents."

"Who does?" Bastille said, her voice flat.

"Well, you *did* say you wanted a bath," Kaz said. "Come on. We should get moving before those knights think to send someone to Keep Smedry."

I sighed, climbing to my feet, and the three of us jogged down the hallway—our clothing making squishing noises—and entered a stairwell. We climbed to the top of one of the keep's towers and ran out onto the landing pad. There we found an enormous glass butterfly lethargically flapping its wings. It reflected the sunlight, throwing out colorful sparkles of light in all directions.

I froze. "Wait. *This* is our escape vehicle?"

"Sure," Kaz said. "*Colorfly*. Something wrong?"

"Well, it's not particularly . . . manly."

"So?" Bastille said, hands on hips.

"Er . . . I mean . . . Well, I was hoping to be able to escape in something a little more impressive."

"So if it's not manly, it's not impressive?" Bastille said, folding her arms.

"I . . . er . . ."

"Now would be a good time to shut up, Al," Kaz said, chuckling. "You see, if your mouth is closed, that will prevent you from saying anything else. And that will prevent you from getting a foot in your mouth—either yours placed there or hers kicking you."

It seemed like good advice. I shut my mouth and trotted after Kaz, making my way to the gangplank up to the glass butterfly.

To this day, however, I'm bothered by that departure. I was going on what was in many ways my first real mission. Before, I'd stumbled into things accidentally. But now I'd actively decided to go out and help.

It seemed that I should be able to make my triumphant departure inside something cooler than a butterfly. In heroic journey terms, that's like being sent to college driving a pale yellow '76 Pacer. (Ask your parents.)

But, as I believe I've proven to you in the past, life is not fair. If life were fair, ice cream would be calorie free, kittens would come with warning labels stamped on their foreheads, and James Joyce's *The Dead* would totally be about zombies. (And don't get me started on Faulkner's *As I Lay Dying*.)

"Hey, cousin!" a voice exclaimed. A head popped out of the bottom of the butterfly. It had short, black hair with dark tan skin. A hand followed, waving at me. Both belonged to a young Mokian girl. If she were from the Hushlands, she'd have been described as Hawaiian or Samoan. She was wear-

ing a colorful red and blue sarong and had a flower pinned in
her hair.

"Who are you?" I asked, walking under the glass vehicle.

"I'm your cousin, Aydee! Kaz says you need me to fly you
to Mokia." There was an exuberance about her that reminded
me of her sister, Australia. Only Australia was much older.
This girl couldn't be more than eight years old.

"*You're* our pilot? But you're just a kid!"

"I know! Ain't it great?" She smirked, then pulled back
into the butterfly, a glass plate sliding into place where she'd
been hanging.

"Best not to challenge her, Al," Kaz said, walking up and
laying a hand on my arm.

"But we're going into a war zone!" I said, looking at Kaz.
"We shouldn't bring a kid into that."

"Oh, so perhaps I should leave *you* behind?" Kaz said.
"The Hushlanders would call you a kid too."

"That's different," I said lamely.

"Her homeland is being attacked," Bastille said, climbing up the gangplank. "She has a right to help. Nobody sends
children into battle, but they can help in other ways. Like
flying us to Mokia. Come on! Have you forgotten that we're
being chased?"

"It seems like I'm *always* being chased," I said, climbing up
the gangplank. "Let's get going."

Kaz followed me up, and the gangplank swung closed. The butterfly lurched into the air and swooped

    ... well, fluttered ...

                    away from the city in a dramatic

    ... well, leisurely ...

        flight toward Mokia, with a dangerous

    ... well, mostly just a *cute* ...

                        determination to see the kingdom protected and defended!

Either that or we'd just spend our time drinking nectar from flowers. You know, whatever ended up working.

Chapter

42

Change.

It's important to change. I, for instance, change my underwear every day. Hopefully you do too. If you don't, please stay downwind.

Change is frightening. Few of us ever want things to change. (Well, things other than underwear.) But change is also fascinating—in fact, it's necessary. Just ask Heraclitus.

Heraclitus was a funny little Greek man best known for letting his brother do all of the hard work, for calling people odd names, and for writing lyrics for Disney songs about two thousand years too early for them to be sung. He was quite an expert on change, even going so far as to change from *alive* to *dead* after smearing cow dung on his face. (Er, yes, that last part is true, I'm afraid.)

Heraclitus is the first person we know of to ever gripe about how often things change. In fact, he went so far as to guess that you can never touch the same object twice—because everything and everybody changes so quickly, any object you touch will change into something else before you touch it again.

I suppose that this is true. We're all made of cells, and those are bouncing around, breaking off, dying, changing. If nothing could change, then we wouldn't be able to think, grow, or breathe. What would be the point? We'd all be about as dynamic as a pile of rocks. (Though, as I think about it, even that pile of rocks is changing moment by moment, as the winds blow and break off atoms.)

So . . . I guess what Heraclitus was saying is that your underpants are always changing, and *technically* you now have on a different pair than you did when you began reading this chapter. So I guess you *don't* have to change them every day.

Sweet! Thanks, philosophy!

I whistled in amazement, hanging upside down from the tree. "Wow! That was *quite* the trip! Aydee, you're a fantastic pilot."

"Thanks!" Aydee said, hanging nearby.

"I mean, I thought thirty-seven chapters' worth of flying would be boring," I said. "But that was probably the most exciting thing I've been a part of since Grandpa showed up on my doorstep six months ago!"

"I particularly enjoyed the fight with the giant half squid, half wombat," Bastille said.

"You really showed him something!" I said.

"Thanks! I didn't realize he'd be so interested in my stamp collection."

"Yeah, I didn't realize you'd taken so many pictures of people's faces you'd stamped on!"

"Personally," Kaz said, untangling himself from the bushes below, "I preferred the part where we flew up into space."

"We should have done that in book two," Bastille said. "Then the cover of the first Hushlands edition would have made sense."

"There were so many exciting things on this trip," I said, still swinging in the vines. "It's tough to pick just one as my favorite."

Kaz dusted himself off, looking up at me. "Reason number eighty-two why it's better to be a short person: When you plummet to your doom, you don't fall as far as tall people."

"What?" I said. "Of course you do!"

"Nonsense," Kaz said. "Maybe our *feet* fall as far as yours, but our heads have less distance to fall. So it's less dangerous for us on average."

"I don't think it works that way," Bastille said.

Kaz shrugged. "Anyway, Al, if you ever write your autobiography, you're going to have a real tough time writing out that trip here. I mean . . . words just won't be able to describe how perfectly *awesome* it was."

"I'm sure I'll think of something," I said, letting Bastille help me untangle myself from the vines. I dropped awkwardly to the ground beside Kaz, and then Bastille went to help Aydee get down.

"Where are we?" I asked.

"Just outside of Tuki Tuki, by my guess," Kaz said. "I'm certain that the rock that knocked down *Colorfly* was thrown by a Librarian machine. I'll go scout for a moment. Wait here."

Kaz moved off into the bushes, pulling out his machete. He didn't—thankfully—engage his Talent. I made sure to keep an eye on him as he walked out toward the sunlit ridge in the near distance. We were in a dense, tropical jungle arrayed with a large number of flowers hanging from vines, sprouting from trees, and blooming at our feet. Insects buzzed around, moving from flower to flower, and didn't seem to have any interest in me or the others.

The flight had taken a long time, but it had seemed to pass

remarkably quickly, considering how busy we'd been with wombats, outer space, and stamp collections. It seemed like just a few moments ago that we'd left Nalhalla, yet now here we were, hours of flying later, in Mokia. In fact, those chapters were so fast, so quick, so exciting, it almost feels like I skipped writing them.

Good thing I didn't, though. That would have been pretty stoopid of me, eh?

Aydee sighed as Bastille helped her down. "I'm going to miss that ship."

"You know," I said, "that's the third time I've been up in one of those glass ships, and it's *also* the third time I've crash-landed. I'm beginning to think that they aren't very safe."

"Of course there *couldn't* be another explanation," Bastille said dryly.

"What do you mean?"

"I've flown in them hundreds of times," Bastille said. "And the only three times *I've* crash-landed, I've been flying with you."

"Oh," I said, scratching my head.

"I'm going to have to travel with you more often, cousin!" Aydee said. "I *never* get shot down when I fly on my own!"

It appeared that Aydee had inherited the characteristic Smedry sense of adventure. I eyed my diminutive cousin. We hadn't had much of a chance to talk, despite the lengthy flight—we'd had to spend too much time dodging war koalas while building a new lighthouse for underprivileged children. (You might want to reread Chapters Five through Forty-One to relive the adventure of it all.)

I reached out to her. "I don't believe I've properly introduced myself. I'm Alcatraz."

"Aydee Ecks," she said energetically. "Is it true you have the Breaking Talent?"

"The one and only," I said. "It's not everything it's cracked up to be."

"No," Bastille added, "*everything else* is what it cracks up."

"What's your Talent?" I asked Aydee, shooting a dry look at Bastille.

"I'm really bad at math!" she proclaimed.

By now I was getting used to Smedry Talents. I'd met family members who were magically bad at dancing, others who were great at looking ugly in the morning. Being bad at math . . . well, that just seemed to fit right in. "Congratulations," I said. "That sounds useful."

Aydee beamed.

Kaz came traipsing back a few moments later, his pack slung on his shoulder. "Yup," he said, "we're here. The capital city is just a short hike down that direction, but there's a full Librarian blockade set up around the place."

"Great," I said.

The others looked to me, expecting me to take the lead. Partially because of my lineage, but also because I'd organized this trip. It was still odd to be in charge, but I'd taken the lead a number of times now. Though it had originally bothered me, I was getting used to it. (Kind of like how listening to really loud music a lot will slowly make your hearing worse.)

"All right," I said, kneeling down. "Let's go over our resources. Bastille, what do you have?"

"Sword," she said, patting the sheath at her side. "Dagger. Warrior's Lenses. Glassweave outfit." Her militaristic trousers and jacket were made of a special kind of defensive glass; they could take a pounding and leave her unharmed. She pulled her stylish sunglasses out of her pocket and put them on. They'd enhance her physical abilities.

"Kaz?"

"I've got a pair of Warrior's Lenses too," he said. He patted his pack. "I've got my sling to throw rocks, and some standard gear. Rope, a couple of throwing knives, a grappling hook, flares, and snacks."

"Snacks?"

"Pop taught me never to rescue a near-doomed allied kingdom on an empty stomach."

"Wise man, my grandfather," I said. "Aydee, what do you have?"

"A bubbly, infectious personality!" she said. "And a cute flower in my hair."

"Excellent." I fished around in my pocket. "I've got my standard Oculator's Lenses," I said, "along with my Translator's Lenses and one Truthfinder's Lens." The former had been given to me by my father; the latter I'd discovered in the tomb of Alcatraz the First. Neither were very powerful in battle, but they could be useful in other ways.

As I fished in the pockets of my jacket, I was shocked to discover something else. A pouch that hadn't been there before, at least not in the morning when I'd gotten dressed. I pulled it out, frowning, then undid the laces at the top.

Inside were two pairs of Lenses. They glowed powerfully to my eyes, as I was wearing my Oculator's Lenses.

I took the new Lenses out. One pair had a baby blue tint to them. I'd used these before; they were called Courier's Lenses. The other Lenses had a green and purple tint.

"Wow," Bastille said, snatching the second pair from my hand, holding them up. "Alcatraz, where did you get *these*?"

"I have no idea," I said, looking inside the pouch. There appeared to be a little note tucked into it. "What are they?"

"Bestower's Lenses," she said, sounding just a bit awed. "They're very powerful."

I got the note out, unfolding it.

You called me once with a set of Courier's Lenses when you weren't supposed to be able to. Give it a try again.

It was signed "Grandpa Smedry."

I hesitated, then pulled off my Oculator's Lenses and put on the Courier's Lenses. They were supposed to be able to work over only short distances, but I was discovering that there were a lot of things about Lenses and silimatic glass that didn't work the way everyone said they did.

I concentrated, doing something I'd only recently learned to do, giving extra *power* to the Lenses. Static fuzzed in my ears. And then an image of Grandpa Smedry's face appeared in front of me, hovering in the air. It was faintly translucent.

Ha! Grandpa's voice said in my ears. *Alcatraz, my boy, you really* can *do it!*

"Yeah," I said. The others gave me odd looks, but I tapped the glasses.

You found the Lenses, I presume? Grandpa asked.

"I did," I replied. "How'd you get them into my pocket?"

Oh, I've been known to practice a little sleight of hand in my day, my boy, he said. *I'd been meaning to give you those Lenses for some time. Make good use of them. I'm sure dear Bastille can tell you how to use them. Ha! The lass seems to know more about my Lenses sometimes than I do! Are you in Mokia yet?*

"We've arrived at Tuki Tuki," I said. "I've got Kaz with me, and my cousin Aydee."

Excellent, lad, excellent. I'm working on the knights. I've almost got them in agreement to come with me to "rescue" you. But they're not convinced that you're in danger. They think that you tricked them and didn't really fly to Mokia—you just acted like it to get them to go join the war.

"Wow," I said. "As I think about it, that might have been a pretty good idea."

Except for the fact that we'll need to prove to them where you are, Grandpa said. *Your cousin Aydee was in town dropping off a bit of Communicator's Glass. The other piece is in the palace, with Bastille's sister, the queen. If you can contact the Mokian embassy in Nalhalla through it, that will prove that you're there in Mokia. They won't take my word on it with the Courier's Lenses, but if you contact the embassy, the knights will have no choice but to come defend you.*

"All right," I said.

This will be dangerous, lad, Grandpa said. *I don't want you getting hurt.*

"But that's the Smedry way!" I said, imitating him.

Ha! Well, so it is. But surviving *is also the Smedry way. Get in, contact the embassy, and then lie low. Don't go fight on the battlefield yourself. Understand?*

"Clear as glass," I said.

What kind of glass? Grandpa asked.

"The transparent kind," I said. "I'll let you know once we're inside."

Good lad.

His face vanished, and I felt an overwhelming fatigue. I stumbled over to a moss-covered stone and sat down, exhausted.

"Alcatraz," Bastille said, "was your grandfather still in Nalhalla?"

I nodded.

"But . . . you shouldn't be able to . . ."

"I know, Bastille," I said. "That's probably why I'm so tired. Impossible things are really rough to do, you know."

She looked troubled.

"Hey!" Kaz exclaimed suddenly, looking through his pack. "I forgot that I stuffed these in here." He pulled out some colored teddy bears.

"Oh!" Aydee said, squealing and running over to snatch them up.

"Aydee!" I said, standing. "Wait! Those are grenades!"

"I know," she said enthusiastically. "I *love* grenades!"

Yes, she's a Smedry all right.

"How many do you have?" I asked.

"One of each of the main three kinds," Kaz said.

"So, six?" Aydee said.

"Uh," I said. "Actually, one plus one plus one is . . ." I trailed off as, suddenly, Aydee was holding not three, but *six* bears.

"One plus one plus one," she proclaimed. "Six, right?"

I blinked. *She's bad at math . . .* Her Talent, it appeared, had *forced* the world to match her powers of addition.

"Don't correct her, Al," Kaz said, chuckling. "At least not when her bad math is in our favor. Nice work, Aydee."

"But what did I do?" she said, confused, handing back the exploding bears.

"Nothing," Kaz said, tucking the bears in his pack.

Aydee was young enough that she hadn't learned to control her Talent yet—and I couldn't really blame her for that, since I barely had my own under control. Her Talent would be hard to control anyway, since she could only make mathematical miracles when she legitimately calculated wrong in her head.

"Alcatraz, are you all right?" Bastille asked.

I nodded, still feeling tired but forcing myself to my feet. "Come on. I want to see what we're up against."

Kaz led the way over to the ridge. We walked up to it, looking out of the jungle over a daunting sight.

Beneath us, the forest had been trampled to the ground. The black tents of an enormous army were pitched amid the stumps of trees, and the smoke of a hundred fires rose into the sky. The army encircled a small hilltop city made entirely of wooden huts, with a wooden-stake wall around the outside. It looked small and fragile, but it had some kind of shield around it—a bubble of glass, like a translucent dome. That glass was cracked and broken in several places.

The army was bad enough. However, the things that stood behind it were even more daunting—three enormous robots dressed like Librarians, holding enormous swords on their shoulders.

"Giant robots," I said. "They have *giant robots.*"

"Er, yes," Kaz said. "That's what threw the rock at us."

"Why didn't anyone shattering *tell* me they had giant robots!"

The others shrugged.

"Maybe we're fighting for the wrong side," I said.

"We're fighting for what is right," Kaz said.

"Yeah, *without* giant robots."

"They're not so tough," Bastille said, eyes narrowed. "They're nearly useless in battle. Always tripping over things."

"But they're great at throwing rocks," Kaz added.

"All right," I said, taking a deep breath. "Grandfather needs us to sneak into the palace and call from inside, using the queen's Communicator's Glass. Any ideas?"

"Well," Kaz said, "I could use my Talent to—"

"No!" Bastille and I both said at the same time. I *still* hadn't gotten all of the dragon stomach snot out of my hair.

"You tall people," Kaz said with a sigh. "Always so paranoid."

"We could steal one of those six robots," Aydee said, thoughtful. "I might be able to pilot one. My training includes Librarian technology."

"That's an idea," I said. "Maybe . . . Wait, *six* robots?"

I looked again, and indeed, where three of the enormous machines had stood, there were now six. A group of Librarians stood around the robots' feet, looking up, seeming confused at where the extra three had come from.

Aydee's Talent, it appeared, could be a liability.

"Great," I said flatly. "Let's ignore the robots for now."

"How are we going to get in, then?" Kaz asked.

I bit my lip in thought. At that point, something deeply profound occurred to me. A majestic plan of beauty and power, a plan that would save us all and Mokia as well.

But, being stoopid, I forgot it immediately. So we did something ridiculous instead.

Chapter

For my plan to work, we had to wait until it grew dark. It was a cold night, chilly, and I stood a lone sentry atop a stone shelf, lost inside my mind. The ghosts of my past seemed, in that caliginous night, to crawl up from the bowels of the earth and whisper to me. At their forefront was the image that I'd once had of my father, my dreams of what he would be when I finally discovered him. A brave man, a man forced to abandon me because of circumstances, not lack of affection. A person I'd be proud to have as my sire.

That man was just illusion. Dead. Killed by the truth that was Attica Smedry. But the ghost whispered at me for vengeance. Whispered at me to . . .

. . . stop being so pretentious.

The above paragraphs are what we authors like to call

literary allusion. That's what we do when we don't know what else to write, so we go and read some other story, looking for great ideas we can steal. However, to avoid *looking* like we're stealing, we leave just enough clues so that someone who is curious can discover the original source. That way, instead of looking like thieves, we instead appear very clever because of the secret meaning we've hidden in our text.

Authors are the only people who get in trouble if they steal from others and try to hide it, but get *praised* for stealing when they do it in the open. Remember that. It'll help you a lot in college.

So, to repeat the previous phrase without the literary allusion: I sat on a rock, waiting for it to get dark, thinking about my stoopid father and how he didn't live up to my expectations. It wasn't actually cold out—Mokia is in the tropics, unlike Denmark. My stomach rumbled; the others were eating some bread and cheese that Kaz had brought, but I didn't feel like eating.

A rustling sound came from behind, and Bastille walked up to my rock, Warrior's Lenses tucked into her jacket pocket. Below, the besieging army was getting ready to camp for the night. I was wearing my Oculator's Lenses—which were also called Primary Lenses, I'd come to learn. They had a reddish tint, and allowed an Oculator to do some very basic things: see auras around types of glass and fight off other Oculators.

Sometimes they let you see other kinds of auras as well, little hints about the world. I wasn't good at using them for that sort of thing yet, though.

Right now, they showed me that the dome around Tuki Tuki was made of a very powerful type of glass. It was in even worse shape than it looked; my Lenses let me see that the aura was wavering. It pulsed with an almost sickly glow. Whatever the Librarians were doing to break down the dome, it was working.

"Hey," Bastille said, sitting down. "What's reflecting?"

"Huh?"

"Free Kingdoms phrase," Bastille said. "It just means 'What are you thinking about?'"

I shrugged.

"It's your parents, isn't it?" Bastille asked. "You always get the same look in your eyes when you think about them."

I shrugged again.

"You're wondering what the point was in rescuing your father, since he didn't end up spending any time with you."

I shrugged, my stomach rumbling again.

Bastille hesitated. "I'm not sure I understood that one. My shrug-ese is kind of rusty."

"I don't know, Bastille," I said, still looking at the city. "It's just that . . . well, I've lost them both. For a few moments we were all there, in the same city. And now I'm alone again."

"You're *not* alone," she said, sitting down on the rock next to me.

"Even when I was with my father, I wasn't *with* him," I said. "He practically ignored me. Every time I tried to talk to him, he acted like I was a bother. He kept sending me off to enjoy myself, offering to give me money, as if the only thing he had to do as a father was provide for me.

"And now they're both gone. And I don't know what any of it was about. They were in love once. When we were captured a few months ago, I watched my mother talk about me to the other Librarians. She said she didn't care about me, but the Truthfinder's Lens said that she was lying."

"Huh," Bastille said. "Well that's good, right? It means she cares."

"It's not good," I said. "It's confusing. It would be so much easier if I could just believe that she hates me. Why did they break up? Why did they think that a Librarian and a Smedry could marry in the first place? And what made them change their minds? Whose fault was it? They were together until I was born . . ."

"Alcatraz," Bastille said. "It's *not* your fault."

I didn't respond.

"Alcatraz . . ."

"I know it's not," I said, mostly to get her to stop prodding me. Bastille fell silent, though I could tell she didn't believe me. She shouldn't have.

I continued staring out into the night. *What is it you're really after, Mother?* I thought. *What is in that book you stole? And why did you lie to the other Librarians about me?*

I'm sorry. Did that last part make you a little depressed? Someone needs to say something funny. How about this: By the end of this book, you'll see me realize that everything I thought I knew about my life was a lie, and I'll be left even more alone than before.

Oh? That wasn't very funny, you say? That's because you didn't hear the joke. I hid it in the sentence, but you have to read it backward to get it.

Did you get it? You might have to read it out loud to sound it out right, if you want to see the joke. Give it a try. Sound out every word.

How was that? What? Oh, that wasn't supposed to make *you* laugh—it was supposed to make everyone around you laugh at how silly you sounded. Did it work? (If you'll look above, I said, 'Someone needs to say something funny,' but I didn't say it would be me. . . .)

"So," Bastille said. "Do you want to know about those Lenses your grandfather gave you?"

"Sure," I said, glad for the change in topic. I pulled out the pair of Bestower's Lenses, with their purple and green tint. When I wore my Primary Oculator's Lenses, the ones in my hand glowed with a strong aura; they were very powerful.

"These are supposed to be tough to use," Bastille said, taking the Bestower's Lenses and inspecting them. "Essentially, they let you give something of yourself to someone else."

"Something?" I asked. "What something?"

She shrugged. "It depends. Like I said, they're hard to use, and nobody seems to understand them perfectly. You put them on, you look at someone and focus on them, then you *send* them something. Some of your strength, something you're feeling, something you can do that they can't. There are reports of strange events tied to this kind of Lens. An Oculator who had hives from a troll allergy once took a set of these and *gave* the hives to his political opponent when she was giving a speech."

"Huh," I said, taking the Lenses back, looking them over.

"Yeah, and since his opponent was a troll herself, it was kind of weird. Anyway, the Lenses are powerful—and dangerous. I'm surprised that your grandfather gave them to you."

"He trusts me more than he should," I said, slipping off my Primary Lenses and putting on the Bestower's Lenses. As always, the tint to the glass was invisible to me once I put the Lenses on.

Bastille jumped as I turned toward her. "Don't point those at me, Smedry!"

"I haven't activated them," I said, my stomach rumbling. I'd need to eat before—

Suddenly I felt full. I cocked my head as Bastille's stomach rumbled.

"Great," she said. "You gave me your hunger. Thanks a lot, Smedry. And I just *ate*."

I felt embarrassed, but Bastille was the one who blushed. I'd given her my embarrassment.

Hurriedly, I pulled the Lenses off. Immediately the effect vanished—I was hungry and embarrassed again. "Wow."

"I *warned* you," Bastille said. "Shattering Glass! You Smedrys never listen." She stormed off, leaving me to sheepishly tuck the Lenses into my pocket again.

Still, they *did* seem like they would be very useful.

I joined the others at our impromptu camp set back from the ridge. "All right," I said, squatting down beside them. "I think it's dark enough. Let's go."

"Sounds good," Kaz said. "What does this plan of yours entail?"

"It's dark," I said.

"And?"

"And so we sneak past the guards and run to the city," I said.

The other three blinked at me. "*That's* your plan?" Kaz said.

"Sure," I replied. "What did you think it was?"

"Something not lame," Aydee said with a frown.

Kaz nodded. "You said you had a plan, and then told us to wait for dark. I figured . . . well, that you'd have something a little more original."

"We could try knocking out guards," I said, "and taking their uniforms."

"I said *more* original," Kaz said.

"What does originality have to do with it?" I asked.

"Everything!" Kaz said, glancing at Aydee, who nodded vigorously. "We're Smedrys! We can't do things the way everyone else does."

"Okay then . . ." I said slowly. "We'll sneak past the guards in the dark, and we'll do it *while quoting Hamlet*."

"Now that's more like it!" Kaz said.

"Never seen anything like it," Aydee added. "It just might be crazy enough to work." She paused. "What's a hamlet?"

"It's a small village," Kaz said.

Bastille rolled her eyes. "I'll go first," she said, slipping on her Warrior's Lenses despite the dark night. "Follow me to the rim of the camp, but don't come any closer until I give the signal."

"Right," I said. "What's the signal?"

"A quote from a hamlet," Kaz said. "Obviously."

"Are you sure a hamlet isn't a very small pig?" Aydee said.

"Nah," Kaz said. "That's a hammer."

Bastille sighed, then hurried off, her dark uniform making her blend into the night. The rest of us followed more slowly, Kaz putting on a pair of rugged, aviator-style sunglasses that were obviously Warrior's Lenses. Aydee got out her own, though hers had yellow rims with flowers painted on them. Uncertain what else to do, I put the Bestower's Lenses back on, though I made certain not to look directly at Kaz or Aydee.

We climbed down from the rim, moving along a game trail through the dense jungle. The Librarian army didn't seem to be anticipating any danger from outside, and most of their attention was focused on Tuki Tuki. Still, guard posts were spaced around the perimeter, each lit by a bonfire. We followed Bastille—who was amazingly quiet as she moved through the underbrush—as she rounded the camp, obviously looking for a place where we could sneak through without causing too much of a disturbance.

She eventually stopped, hiding in the shadows just outside the camp near a watch fire that had been allowed to burn low. It was mostly just coals now, a couple of tired-looking Librarian guards standing watch. They were beefy men, the type with square jaws and stoopid names like Biff, Chad, or Brandon. They had on white shirts with pocket protectors and pink bow ties, but had enormously strong bodies. Like some-one had combined a math nerd and a football player into one unholy hybrid.

Bastille took a deep breath, then dashed across the trampled ground with blurring speed. The Librarians barely had time to stand up straight and squint into the darkness before she was upon them.

Now, in case you somehow slept through the other three books, let me explain something. Bastille is *fast*. Like cheetah-on-a-sugar-buzz fast. She not only has those Warrior's Lenses, but she's also a Crystin. Every Knight of Crystallia has a little crystal grown into the skin at the back of their neck. That crystal comes from the Worldspire and connects every Crystin to all of the others. They all share a little of their skills and abilities with the other knights.

This, in turn, makes every shattering one of them crazy insane supersoldiers, even the thirteen-year-old girls. *Especially* the thirteen-year-old girls. (Every teenage girl has a crazy insane supersoldier inside of them, waiting to get out. If you don't believe me, it probably means you don't have any teenage sisters. Particularly not two who both want to wear the same necklace to the prom.)

Bastille didn't even need to get out her sword. She made the first guard double over with a punch to the stomach, then grabbed his shoulder and used it to steady herself as she spun,

kicking the other guard in the neck and dropping him to the ground. She followed this by punching the first guard square in the forehead.

Both men fell to the ground, silent. Bastille glanced back toward where we were hiding. "I think we ought to get our roads cobbled!" she whispered. Then—I could see her sighing visibly—she added, "Oink oink oink."

I smiled as the three of us trotted up to the watch fire. Kaz had out his sling, but hadn't needed it. The two guards were out cold. Bastille waited, tense, glancing toward the two nearest watch fires—in the distance to either side of us. The guards at them didn't seem to have noticed us.

"Nice work, Bastille," Kaz said, inspecting the guards and setting aside their futuristic rifles. Most Free Kingdomers didn't find guns and other "primitive" weapons to be very useful.

I, on the other hand, had watched enough action movies to know that if you're going to sneak through the middle of an enemy army, a gun can be a pretty cool thing to have. So I reached down and picked up one of the rifles.

"Alcatraz!" Bastille said. "Put that down! Your Talent!"

"Don't worry," I said. "I've learned to control it. Look, the gun isn't even falling apart."

Indeed, it remained in one perfect piece. Bastille relaxed as I lifted the gun, placing it against my shoulder, barrel toward the air.

And—as if to prove me wrong—I felt a little jolt as my Talent was engaged. The gun didn't fall apart, however.

It just fired. Shooting directly into the air with an extremely loud cracking noise, blasting a glowing ball of light into the sky.

Shocked, I dropped the gun. It hit the ground, going off again, shooting another glowing ball out into the forest.

The black night was completely still for a moment. And then a loud blaring alarm noise began to echo through the camp.

"Frailty," Bastille said with a sigh, "thy name is Alcatraz."

° Scene iii °

The following chapter introduction is an excerpt from Alcatraz Smedry's best-selling book, *How to Sound Really Smart in Three Easy Steps.*

STEP ONE: Find an old book that everyone has heard of but nobody has read.

The clever writers know that literary allusions are useful for lots of reasons other than giving you stuff to write when you run out of ideas. They can also make you look *way* more important. What better method to seem intelligent than to include an obscure phrase in your story? It screams, "Look how smart I am. I've read lots of old books."

STEP TWO: Skim through that old play or document until you find a section that makes no sense whatsoever.

Shakespeare is great for this for one simple reason: *None* of what he wrote makes any sense at all. Using confusing old phrases is important because it makes you look mysterious. Plus, if nobody knows what the original author meant, then they can't complain that you used the phrase wrong. (Shakespeare, it should be noted, was paid by other authors to write gibberish. That way when they wanted to quote something that didn't make sense, they just had to reach for one of his plays.)

STEP THREE: Include a quote from that play or old document in an obvious place, where people will think they're smart for spotting it.

Note that you get bonus points for changing a few of the words to make a clichéd turn of phrase, as it will stick in people's minds that way. Reference the last sentence of the previous chapter for an example.

Also note that if you aren't familiar with Shakespeare, you can always use Greek philosophers instead. Nobody knows what the heck *they* were talking about, so using them in your books is a great way to pretend to be smart.

Everybody wins!

"O horrible, O horrible, most horrible!" Kaz cried as the alarm went off.

"Why," Aydee said. "What should be the fear?"

"More matter," Bastille said, pointing at the glass dome of the city, then pulling out her sword. "With *less art*."

"Bid the players make haste!" I cried, dashing away from the fallen gun. We took off at a run toward Tuki Tuki.

All around us, the camp was coming alert. Fortunately, they didn't know what the disturbance was or what had caused it. Many of the Librarians seemed to assume that the shot had come from the besieged city, and they were forming up battle lines facing the dome. Others were running toward the place where the shot I'd fired had entered the jungle.

"If there be any good thing to be done . . ." Bastille said, looking about, worried.

The scrambling soldiers gave me an idea. Up ahead, I saw a gun rack where a bunch of rifles leaned, waiting to be picked up by Librarians for battle. I waved to the others, racing toward the rack. I ran past it, fingers brushing the weapons and engaging my Talent. They all fired, shooting glowing shots up into the air, arcing over the camp and furthering the chaos.

"What a piece of work is a man!" Kaz called, giving me a thumbs-up.

Librarian soldiers ran this way and that, confused. Amid them were men and women dressed in all black—stark black uniforms for the men, with black shirts and ties, and black skirts with black blouses for the women. Some of these noticed my group running through camp and began to cry out, pointing at us.

Aydee yelped suddenly, pointing ahead of us. "Something is rotten in the state of Denmark!"

Indeed, a group of soldiers had noticed us and—spurred by the Librarians in black—was sprinting for us.

There wasn't much time to think. Bastille charged them at the head, of course. She wouldn't be able take them all though. There were too many.

Kaz raised his sling, whipping a rock at a Librarian. The man dropped like Polonius in Act III, Scene iv, but there were still a good ten Librarians to fight. Kaz kept slinging rocks as Bastille surged into the middle of them, sword out and raised before her. Aydee hid behind some barrels at a command from Kaz.

And me. What could I do? I stood there in the chaotic

night, trying to decide. I was the leader of this expedition. I needed to help *somehow*!

A Librarian soldier came rushing at me, crying, "Let me be cruel, not unnatural!" He carried a sword; obviously these men were ready to deal with Smedrys, just in case. A gun would have been useless against my Talent.

I stepped back nervously. What could I do? Break the ground beneath him? That might as easily toss me into the hole, as well as the others. Hurting myself in the process wouldn't . . .

Something occurred to me.

Without bothering to consider whether it was a good idea, I focused on the man, activating my Lenses. Then I punched myself in the head.

Now, under normal circumstances this kind of activity should be frowned upon. In fact, punching yourself in the head

is most definitely what we call stoopiderific (defined as "the level of stoopidity required to go slip-n-sliding at the Grand Canyon"). However, in this case it was slightly less stoopiderific.

The Bestower's Lenses transferred the punch from me to the Librarian. He was suddenly knocked sideways, looking more shocked than hurt.

He stumbled to his feet. "O, what a rogue and peasant slave am I."

"There is nothing either good or bad," I noted, smiling. "But *thinking* makes it so." I punched myself in the stomach as hard as I could.

The Librarian grunted, stumbling again. I went at it over and over, until he was groaning and in no shape to get back up. I looked around, scanning the chaotic grounds of the fight. People were running everywhere. Kaz was standing atop the barrels that Aydee was hiding behind, and she'd brought out a few of the teddy bear grenades. I just managed to dodge to the side as she pulled the tag on a blue one and tossed it at some nearby Librarians, causing them to reverse explode toward each other in a lump.

I picked another Librarian running by and began to pound on him by pounding on myself. However, I wasn't avoiding damage entirely. In fact, when I stopped focusing on Librarians I'd pummeled, the pains started to come back to me. I needed a different method.

"Thou wretched, rash, intruding fool, farewell!" a Librarian cried, dashing toward me.

I spun, focusing on him, and did the first thing I could think of. I pretended that I was crazy. *I'm insane, I'm insane, I'm insane!* I thought.

The man hesitated, lowering his sword. He cocked his head, then wandered away. "Do you see yonder cloud that's almost in shape of a camel?" he asked, glancing at the sky.

Bastille was in the center of a furious battle. She tried not to hurt people too much, but there was no helping it here. She'd had to stab several of the Librarians, and they lay on the ground holding leg or arm wounds. One man, shockingly, had been stabbed in the mouth. He clutched something in his hand, and as I ran past him, he mumbled, "But break, my heart, for I must hold my tongue. . . ."

"O, woe is me," I said, squeezing my eyes shut, "to have seen what I have seen, see what I see!"

I couldn't leave my eyes closed for long though. I opened them, trying to get close to Bastille to help. She seemed to be holding out well. One Librarian came up behind her, trying to attack her from the side. He jumped at her, joined by a group of friends, grabbing her arm and knocking her large, crystal sword out of her hand.

"O, what a noble mind is here o'erthrown!" I yelled, pointing.

Kaz glanced toward us and nodded, grabbing a pink bear from Aydee and tossing it in our direction. It struck, blowing all of us backward. I hit the ground in a roll, but like before the grenade didn't actually hurt any of us.

That explosion was enough to get Bastille free from her grapplers, but her sword had been knocked away. I scrambled to get it for her as she pulled her dagger from her belt, facing down a Librarian.

"Is this a dagger which I see before me?" the Librarian said, holding up a larger, much more imposing sword. He swung.

Bastille just smiled, blocking his sword with her dagger, then stepping unexpectedly forward and kicking him in the crotch with a booted foot.

"Get thee to a nunnery," she said as he squeaked and fell to the ground.

Bastille *hates* it when people quote from the wrong play.

I grabbed Bastille's sword, then dashed toward her, tossing it into her hands as I passed. "Neither a borrower nor a lender be: For loan oft loses both itself and friend."

"Beggar that I am, I am even poor in thanks," she said with an appreciative nod.

I looked about for more enemies. Shockingly, most of the Librarians in this group were down.

"Will you two help to hasten them?" Kaz yelled, running

past us, Aydee at his side. "Rich gifts wax poor when givers prove unkind!"

I nodded in agreement, bolting toward the far side of the camp. Oddly, as we ran, we passed heaped-up piles of what appeared to be glass. Cups, mirrors, windows—all broken, many so badly that they were nearly unrecognizable. I didn't have much energy to ponder on the oddity though. Using the Bestower's Lenses had taken a lot out of me—my stomach hurt from being punched so often, and the Lenses had sapped away a lot of my strength.

Fortunately, the Librarians were confused enough by the nighttime attack that we were able to run the rest of the distance without being stopped again. We burst out of the camp and ran up the hillside toward the glass-domed city above. Behind, Librarians shouted, some pointing at us. A rank of riflemen set up to shoot us down, but they made the mistake of pointing at not one, but *three* Smedrys. Three of the riflemen got lost while trying to raise their guns, five miscounted and didn't put any bullets in their guns, and the rest of the weapons fell apart as their owners tried to use them.

Sometimes it's good to have a Talent.

Unfortunately, I hadn't considered how we were going to get *into* the city once we reached it. The glass dome ran all the way down to the ground, and although there appeared to be a place where hinges made a glass door, that was guarded by a group of Mokian soldiers. The stout, well-muscled men were bare-chested, their faces painted with black swirling lines and patterns like Maori war paint. They carried spears made from a black wood, and some of the spearheads were on fire.

Despite the fearsome display, the soldiers looked like they'd had a hard time of it in the fighting. Most of them wore bandages or slings, and they regarded me and my group with suspicion.

"Our purpose may hold there!" one of the men said through a small slit in the glass. "Who comes here?" They didn't open the door for us.

I stepped forward. "Sir, my good friend. I do commend me to you."

Bastille also stepped forward, showing her Crystin blade, the symbol of a Knight of Crystallia. "Swear by my sword," she proclaimed.

A Crystin seemed enough proof for the Mokians that we were good guys. They opened the small glass doorway, waving us in. We let Kaz and Aydee go first while I looked back at the camp. We'd done it! I puffed in fatigue, but smiled at our victory.

Beside me, Bastille seemed less enthusiastic.

"How is it that the clouds still hang on you?" I asked her.

She shrugged, regarding the chaotic Librarian ranks, particularly the place where we'd been forced to fight. "My soul is full of discord and dismay."

"The lady doth protest too much, methinks."

Bastille looked at me. I could tell from her expression that she blamed me for upsetting everything. That was probably fair, since I'd not only been the one to suggest the plan, but the one to ruin it by picking up the Librarian's gun.

"How absolute the knave is," Bastille said, tapping me on the chest.

"This above all," I said, shrugging and smiling wryly, "to thine own self be true."

And with that, we entered Tuki Tuki.

Chapter

A+

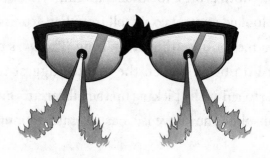

AAAAAAAAAAAAAAAAAAAAAAAAAAAAAAAA
AAAAAAAAAAAAAAAAAAAAAAAAAAAAAAAA
AAAAAAAAAAAAAAAAAAAAAAAAAAAAAAAA
AAAAAAAAAAAAAAAAAAAAAAAAAAAAAAAA
AAAAAAAAAAAAAAAAAAAAAAAAAAAAAAAA
AAAAAAAAAA!!!!!!!!!!!!!!!

. . .

AAAAAAAAAAAAAAAAAAAAAAAAAAAAAAAA
AAA!!!!!!!!!!!!!

The Mokian soldiers ushered us through the glass doorway, several of them keeping watchful guard at the army
behind. Inside the glass shield, a ten-foot-high wooden wall
surrounded the city. The wall was battered and broken,

burned in places, and looked like it had seen a lot of fighting before the glass dome had been put in place.

As soon as we were through the door, several soldiers slammed it shut. One of the soldiers called up toward the wall. "Smedrys have arrived! A Crystin is with them! Lady Aydee has returned!"

Others picked up the shouts, passing them along the line of ragged defenders standing atop the wall. The men around me lost their suspicion and began to look hopeful.

"Lord Smedry," one of them said. "You are an advance force? How many troops is Nalhalla sending us?"

"Are there any others with you?" another asked hopefully.

"Are the Knights of Crystallia mobilized?" yet another asked. "When will they arrive?"

"Er," I said, taking off my Bestower's Lenses as more questions swarmed me.

"We're alone," Bastille said curtly. "We didn't bring any more help, the knights aren't mobilized, and we really don't have time to talk about it."

Everyone fell silent. Bastille has a talent for killing conversations. Basically, Bastille has a talent for killing anything.

"What she means," I said, shooting a glare in her direction, "is that we're here to help, and we hope more will follow. But we're it for now."

The soldiers seemed crestfallen.

"I'm sorry we didn't let you in more quickly, Lord Smedry," said one of the men. "It seemed like you had young Aydee captive, and we weren't sure what was going on."

Oh, right, I thought. *It probably would have made sense to have her approach first, since she's from the city.* Ah well. You can't expect me to think of everything, particularly considering how stoopid I am.

You haven't forgotten that, have you? Don't make me start spelling things wrong to prove it to you.

In the distance, a gate opened in the wooden wall and a contingent of Mokians came out carrying spears that were alight with fire in the night. The soldiers around us made way for the newcomers, and I could tell they respected the man at their lead. He was tall, with long black hair pulled into a ponytail and tied with a beaded string. His face was painted with black lines. He had a powerful, muscular chest and— like most of the other Mokians—wore a simple wrap around his waist, colored red and blue. For some reason, he looked vaguely familiar to me.

"So it is true," he said, stopping before us, burning spear held to the side. "Welcome, Lord Alcatraz Smedry, to our doomed city. You have picked an interesting time to visit us. Lady Bastille, your sister will be pleased to see you, though I doubt the circumstances will make her happy. Lord Kazan, you are welcome—as always—in Tuki Tuki."

"Do I know you?" Kaz said, narrowing his eyes.

"I'm general of the city guard in Tuki Tuki," the man said. He had a commanding, deep voice. "I have seen you many times, though I doubt I was worth your notice. Likely you have seen my face, but we have never been introduced." He looked to Aydee and nodded to her. "Child, your brave mission does you honor. We are already in communication with the embassy in Nalhalla."

Aydee blushed. "Thank you, Your . . . er . . . General Mallo."

"We had not expected you to return, however," he said sternly. "You should have remained in Nalhalla, where it is safe."

Her blush deepened. "But my cousin needed a pilot! He had to come to Mokia!"

"Yes," Mallo said flatly. "I've received a report from the embassy regarding the urgent departure. A vacation to visit the mud baths? That is ridiculous, even for a Smedry."

Now it was my turn to blush. "General," I said, "there are other reasons for our visit. I need to speak to the queen as soon as possible—and after that, I'll need a little time with your Communicator's Glass. I might be able to get you some help for this siege."

The soldiers nearby perked up, and the general gave me an appraising look. "Very well. The Smedry clan has long been friends, and sometimes family, of the Mokian royalty. You are always welcome." He gathered some soldiers, then led us to the city gate.

"I feel I should give you some kind of grand introduction, Lord Smedry," General Mallo said as we entered Tuki Tuki. "But these are not days for joyful tours. So instead, just let me say this. Welcome to the City of Flowers." He raised a hand as I stepped through the gate.

We were at the bottom of the gentle hillside. I looked up along the main road that ran all the way to the palace. Flowers grew on virtually everything. The hutlike buildings were overgrown with vines that intertwined with the reeds that made up their walls, and these sprouted colorful, hibiscus-like blossoms. Flowerbeds ran alongside the road, with exotic bird-of-paradise blooms perching atop them. A line of enormous trees ran behind the buildings, their limbs extending out over the rooftops. These grew heaps of purple flowers that hung down over the road, collected in bunches like grapes. It was gorgeous.

"Wow," I said. "Glad I'm not allergic!"

General Mallo grunted, gesturing with his flaming spear, leading us forward. Carrying that spear around struck me as a little bit dangerous, but who was I to speak? After all, I was

the one walking around with a weapons-grade Smedry Talent stuffed inside me.

"Fortunately, Lord Smedry," Mallo said as we walked, "our flowers are all nonallergenic."

"How did you get them that way?" I asked.

"We asked them very nicely," Mallo said.

"Er, okay."

"It was much more difficult than it sounds, Alcatraz," Aydee added. "Do you know how many different species of flower there are in the city? Six thousand! Our floralinguists had to learn each and every language."

"Floralinguists?" I said.

"They talk to flowers!" Aydee said excitedly.

"I kind of figured that," I said. "What kinds of things do they say?"

"Oh," Mallo said, "they tend to ramble a lot and use big words, but there isn't often much substance to what they say, despite the beauty and ornamentation of the language."

"So . . . er . . ." I said.

"Yeah," Mallo said. "Their speech is quite flowery."

I walked right into that one like a bird hitting a glass sliding door at seventy miles an hour. Beside me, Bastille rolled her eyes.

Kaz whistled, watching the city. "There are more things in heaven and earth . . . er, sorry. I'm having trouble getting over that last chapter. Anyway, I've always loved visiting Tuki Tuki. There's no place like it; I always forget how beautiful it is."

"Perhaps it was a pleasure to visit in the past," Mallo said, his face growing even more solemn, "but the siege has been difficult for all of us. See how our regal daftdonias droop? The Shielder's Glass lets in light, but the plants can feel that they are enclosed. The entire city wilts beneath the Librarian oppression."

Indeed, many of the flowers lining the street did seem to be drooping. As the wonder of my first sight of Tuki Tuki began to wear off, I saw many other signs of the siege. Open yards where people were up despite the late hour, cutting bandages and boiling them in enormous vats. The sounds of blacksmiths working on weapons rang in the air. Most of the men we passed—and many of the women—wore bandages and carried weapons. Spears with long, shark-tooth-like ridges down the sides, or swords and axes of wood, also made with shark-tooth sides.

If you're wondering where the Mokians get all of those shark teeth, by the way, it involves using children as bait—specifically children who skip to the ends of books to read the last page first. I'm sure that *you* would never do something like that. That would be downright stoopiderific.

Many of those passing waved hello to Aydee, and she

waved back. Her family, the Mokian Smedrys, were well known. Eventually we approached the palace. It looked like a very large hut, constructed using thick reeds for the walls. It had a crown of red flowers blanketing its thatch roof.

Now, you're probably thinking what I am. Huts? Aren't the Mokians supposed to be one of the most learned, scientifically minded people in the Free Kingdoms? What were they doing living in huts?

I assumed that, obviously, there was a good explanation. "So, these buildings," I said. "They're made of special, reinforced magical reeds, I assume. They *look* like huts, but they're as strong as castles, right?"

"No," Mallo said. "They're just huts."

"Oh. But they've got Expander's Glass inside of them, right? They look small from the outside, but they're enormous on the inside?"

"No. They're just huts."

I frowned.

"We like huts," Mallo said, shrugging. "Sure, we could build skyscrapers or castles. But why? To cut ourselves off from the sky with walls of stone and steel?"

"It makes sense," Bastille added. "Huts *are* more advanced than the buildings you have in the Hushlands, Smedry. Automatic air-conditioning, for one thing, and—"

"No," Mallo said. "With all respect, young knight, we must

learn to stop saying things like this. We like to pretend that what *we* have is better than what the Librarians have. But comparisons like those, and the jealousy they inspire, began this war in the first place."

He looked forward, toward the palace. "We choose this life in Mokia. Not because it is 'primitive' or 'advanced,' but because it is what we like. The more complex the things surrounding your life become—the homes, the vehicles, the things you put in your homes and your vehicles—the more time you must spend on them. And the less time you have for thought and study."

I blinked, shocked to hear those words coming from the mouth of the enormous, spear-wielding, war-painted Mokian. To the side, Bastille folded her arms, brooding. Her assertions that everything in the Free Kingdoms was better than things in the Hushlands had shocked me the first day we met. I had assumed that was the way all Free Kingdomers thought, but I was coming to realize that Bastille just has a . . . particular way of seeing the world.

(That means that she's bonkers. But I can't *write* that she's bonkers, because if I do, she'll punch me. So, uh, perhaps we should forget I wrote this part, eh?)

We reached the steps up to the palace, where a woman waited for us. She looked familiar too, though this time I could pinpoint why. She looked a lot like her sister, Bastille.

Tall and slender, Angola Dartmoor was about ten years older than Bastille and wore a Mokian wrap of yellow and black with a matching flower in her hair. She carried a royal scepter of ornately carved wood.

She was absolutely beautiful. She had long blonde hair, kind of the shade of a bowl of mac and cheese. She was smiling a wide, genuine smile—which was rather the shape of a macaroni and cheese noodle. She seemed to radiate light, much like a bowl of mac and cheese might if you stuffed a lightbulb into it. Her skin was soft and squishy, like—

Okay. Maybe I'm too hungry to be writing right now. Either way though, Angola was *gorgeous*. Definitely one of the most beautiful women I'd ever seen.

Bastille stepped on my foot.

"Ow!" I complained. "What was that for?"

"Stop gawking at my sister," Bastille grumbled.

"I wasn't gawking! I was *appreciating*!"

"Well, appreciate her a little less, then. And stop drooling."

"I'm not—" I cut off as Angola breezed down the steps gracefully, coming up to us. "I'm not drooling," I hissed more softly, then bowed. "Your Majesty."

"Lord Smedry!" she said. "I've heard so much about you!"

"Er . . . you have?"

She didn't reply, instead laying her hands gracefully on her sister's shoulders. "And Bastille. After all these months of writing you and asking you to visit, now you finally come? During a siege? I should have known that only danger would lure you. Sometimes I wonder if you're not as attracted to it as those you protect!"

Bastille blushed.

"Come," Angola said. "You are welcome to what comforts Mokia can provide you. We will take morning repast and discuss the news you bring. The Aumakua bless that it be of good report, as we have seen too little of that as of late."

Now, as an aside, you might be shocked to hear such a distinct reference to religion from Angola. After all, I haven't talked much about religion in these books.

This is intentional, mostly from a self-preservation standpoint. I've discovered that talking about religion has a lot in common with wearing a catcher's mask: both give people liberty to throw things at you. (And in the case of religion, sometimes the "things" are lightning bolts.)

Unfortunately, in the later years of my life I've developed a very rare affliction known as chronic smart-aleckiness. (It's kind of like dyslexia, only easier to spell. Particularly if you don't have dyslexia.) Because of this tragic, terminal disease, I'm unable to read or write about things without making stoopid wisecracks about them.

Because of my affliction, I've wisely left the topic of religion alone—because if I were to talk about it, I'd have to make fun of it. And that might be offensive, as people take their religions very seriously. Better not to talk about it at all.

Therefore, I will most certainly *not* tell you what religion has in common with explosive vomiting. (Whew. Glad I didn't say anything like that. It could have been *really* offensive.)

Angola nodded to Kaz and Aydee in welcome, giving each a smile, then glided back up the steps, expecting us to follow her in.

"Wow," I said. "Is she always so . . ."

"Nauseatingly regal?" Bastille asked softly. "Yeah, even before she was married."

"Well, I can see why the king married her. Too bad I won't be able to meet him."

Bastille's eyes flickered toward Mallo. It was only for a moment, but I caught it. Frowning, I turned to study the general, trying to find out what had drawn Bastille's attention. Once again, he looked familiar to me. In fact . . .

"You're the king!" I exclaimed, pointing at him.

"What?" Mallo said, voice stiff. "No I'm not. The king was taken to safety by the Knights of Crystallia weeks ago."

He was a terrible liar.

"Hey," Kaz said. "Yeah, I *thought* I recognized you. Your Majesty! We had dinner once a few years back. Remember? My father spilled cranberry juice on your tapa."

The man looked embarrassed. "Perhaps we should go inside," he said. "I see there are some things I need to explain."

(Also, if you're wondering, it's because both often make you fall to your knees.)

Chapter

° No! °

I try very hard to be deep, poignant, and meaningful at the beginning of each chapter. Most of the content of these books is basically silliness. (Granted, these events are real silliness that actually *happened* to me, but that doesn't stop them from being silly.) In the introductions, therefore, I feel it's important to explain meaningful and important concepts so that your time reading won't be completely wasted.

I suggest you scrutinize these introductions, searching for their hidden meanings. My thoughts will bring you enlightenment and wisdom. If you are confused by something I say, rest assured that I'll eventually explain myself.

For instance, in reading the introduction to the previous chapter, you might have understood my screams to be an expression of the existential angst felt by modern teens when thrust into a world they were ill-prepared to receive— a world that has changed so drastically from the one their parents knew. (Thanks for nothing, Heraclitus!) Or you might have seen it as the scream of one realizing that nobody can offer him help or succor.

(In fact, I wrote *that* introduction to express the existential crisis I felt when an enormous spider crawled up my leg while I was typing. But you get the idea.)

We stepped into the palace. It smelled of reeds and thatch, and the wide, open windows let in a cool breeze. The rug was made of long, woven leaves, and the furniture was constructed of tied bundles of reeds. Quite cozy, assuming you weren't enraged, confused, and feeling betrayed like I was.

"You knew," I said, pointing at Bastille.

"I recognized His Majesty immediately," she admitted. "But he seemed to want to keep his identity secret. So I played along."

"I did too," Aydee said. "I . . . er, just didn't do a very good job of it. Sorry."

"It's all right," said Mallo, also known as King Talaki-mallo of Mokia. His wife stepped up beside him, and the guards watched the doorway into the palace.

"But why hide from me?" I asked.

"And me!" Kaz said, folding his arms, stepping up beside me.

"It wasn't just from you," the king said. "It was from all outsiders. You see, we sort of . . . well, tricked the knights."

Bastille raised an eyebrow.

"They insisted that I be protected," Mallo said, voice fervent. "They *would not* stop pestering me. I worried they'd kidnap me and take me from the city for my own good."

"The city is close to falling, Your Majesty," Bastille said. "Mokia can't afford for the entire royal family to be taken by the Librarians. What of the rest of the kingdom? It will need leadership."

"There *is* no 'rest of the kingdom,' child," Mallo said. "Mokia stands here. We've been beaten down by Librarian forces for decades now; if Tuki Tuki falls, it will spell the end for my people. We will become just another Librarian province, slowly assimilated into the Hushlands, our people brainwashed until we forget our past."

The queen laid a hand on her husband's arm. "We are not ignorant of the importance of preserving the royal lineage, fair sister—if only so that a proper resistance can be mounted to reclaim Mokia, should that become our fate."

Before you ask, *yes*, she actually talks like that. I once asked her to pass the butter and she said, "It pleases me to bequeath this condiment unto you, young Alcatraz." Really. No kidding.

"But wait," I said, scratching my head. Being stoopid, I do that a lot. "You're here, but the knights think that you're safe somewhere else?"

"Our daughter imitated me," Mallo said. "She is an Oculator and has a pair of Disguiser's Lenses. The knights shepherded her away to a hidden location while she used her Lenses to appear as if she were me."

"The lineage is safe," Angola said.

"And I can stay to fight with my people, as is right." Mallo looked grim. "Rather, I can fall with my people. I'm afraid that several Smedrys and a single knight will not be enough to win this siege. Our Shielder's Glass is nearly broken, and most of my warriors have fallen to comas in battle. Those who remain have taken many wounds. My silimatic scientists think that one more day of fighting will shatter the dome. We are faced by superior numbers and superior firepower. In the moments before you arrived, I had made the difficult decision to surrender. I was on my way to the wall to announce it to the Librarians."

The words hung in the air like a foul stench—the kind that everyone notices but doesn't want to point out, for fear of being named the one who caused it.

Well, guess we came here for nothing, I thought. *We should probably turn around and get out of here.*

"I'm here to help, Your Majesty," I said instead. "And I

can bring others. If you will resist a little longer, I will not let Mokia fall."

I'm not sure where the brave words came from. Perhaps a smarter man would have known not to say them. Even as they came out of my mouth, I was shocked by my stoopidity. Remember what I said about bravery?

Ridiculous though the proclamation was, the king did not laugh. "I have found that the word of a Smedry is like gold, young Alcatraz," King Mallo said appraisingly. "Of great value, but sometimes easy to bend. Are you certain you can bring aid to my people?"

No.

"Yes," I said.

The king studied me, then glanced at his wife.

"If we surrender, our people retain their lives," Angola said, "but lose their *selves*. If there remains but a slim chance . . ."

He nodded in agreement. "You said you needed to use our Communicator's Glass, Alcatraz. Let us see what you can do with it, and then I will judge."

* * *

"Are you certain this is the right thing to do?" Bastille hissed to me.

We sat on a wicker bench, waiting as the king and his wife fetched the Communicator's Glass. Aydee was talking to one of the soldiers, getting news about her family. (Sing, Australia, and their parents had been sent to provide leadership at the other main battlefront in the Mokian war—though I suspect that the king really sent them away to prevent them from being captured when the city fell.) Kaz stood nearby, arms folded as he leaned against the wall, wearing his brown leather jacket and aviator sunglasses.

"I don't know if this is right," I admitted to Bastille. "But we can't just let them give up."

"If they fight, people will get hurt," Bastille said, leaning in close to me. "Can we really offer them enough hope to justify that? Now that I've seen how bad it is, I don't know if even the full force of the Knights of Crystallia would be enough to turn this war around."

"I . . ." I trailed off, growing befuddled. I did that frequently when Bastille sat really close to me, particularly when I could smell the scent of the shampoo in her hair. Shouldn't girls smell like flowers or something like that? Bastille just smelled like soap.

It was strangely intoxicating anyway. Obviously she gives off some kind of brain-clouding radiation. That's the only explanation.

"Shattering Glass, what am I saying?" she said, pulling back. "Of *course* it's better for them to fight! I'm sorry. I've just grown so used to contradicting you on principle that I'm shocked when you do something smart."

"Duurrr . . ." I said.

She narrowed her eyes at me. "You aren't still mooning over my sister, are you?" Her voice was quite threatening.

I shook out of my stupor. "What? No. Don't be stoopid."

"Did you just call me stoopid?"

"No, I told you not to be stoopid. What is it with you and your sister, anyway?"

"Nothing! I love my sister. We're like two shattering flowers in a field of shattering daisies."

"What does that even mean?"

"I don't know! It was supposed to sound sisterly or something."

I snorted in derision.

"So what's *that* supposed to mean?" Bastille demanded. "I'm *very* affectionate with my sister!"

"So much so that you've never visited her in Mokia?"

"It's a long way away, and I was busy training to become a knight. So that I could keep idiots like *you* out of trouble!"

"Wait. You get mad when I *imply* that you might be stoopid, but it's all right for you to call me an idiot?"

"Because you're a Smedry!"

"That's always your excuse," I said. "I don't buy it. Besides, this time you said you agreed with what I was doing!"

"So!"

"So!"

"So?"

"So maybe we should, like, go catch a movie together or something," I said, standing up. "Sometime when we're not being chased by Librarians or being eaten by dragons or things like that!"

Bastille paused, cocking her head, frowning. "Wait. What?"

I found myself blushing. Why had I said *that*? I mean, I'd been thinking about it for a while, but . . .

Brain-clouding radiation. Obviously.

"It was nothing," I said, panicking. "I just, uh, got confused, and—"

"What's a 'movie'?" she asked. "And why would we need to catch it? Did one escape?"

"Er, yes. They're these big, monstrous creatures that the Librarians let loose in the Hushlands. To terrorize people . . . and, you know, and steal their time, and make them cringe at bad acting, and then make them sit through long boring award shows that give statues of little gold men to people you've never heard of."

She frowned even further. "You're an idiot sometimes, Smedry," she said, then glanced at Kaz, as if asking for an explanation from him.

"I'm not *touching* this one," he said, smiling. "In fact, I'm staying so far away from it, I might as well be in the next king-dom over!"

"Whatever," Bastille said, turning her narrowed eyes back on me—as if she suspected that I was making fun of her in some way she couldn't figure out. I just continued to blush, right up until the point where Mallo and Angola returned. The queen carried a small hand mirror. She crossed the woven rug and handed it to me.

I hesitated, looking down at the mirror. Half of the glass was missing. "This is it?"

"Communicator's Glass is best if portable," Mallo said. "We broke this piece in half and sent it to Nalhalla; it will allow us to communicate for some weeks through the two pieces, until the power fades. Then the glass must be reforged and broken again. It's not the easiest way to talk across a distance, but we were desperate, particularly after sending away our last Oculator to maintain my disguise."

"Librarian agents destroyed our other means of communication," one of the soldiers added. "The Transporter's Glass station, the soundrunners, even the city's stockpile of Messenger's Glass."

I frowned. "How'd they do that?"

"They continue to dig tunnels into the city," Mallo said with a sigh. "And send strike teams up to harry us. We just caught one earlier today. We captured them before they could do any permanent damage, then collapsed the tunnel. There will be more, however."

I nodded, raising the hand mirror. They all looked at me expectantly, as if they figured that—being an Oculator—I'd immediately know how to use the glass. "Um," I said, turning it sideways. "Er. Mirror, mirror, in my hand, my food is tasty, but often bland."

"Alcatraz?" Kaz asked. "What are you doing? You just have to touch the glass to make it work."

"Oh," I said, tapping the mirror. It shimmered, like I'd disturbed the top of a crystal-clear pool of water. A moment later,

the image changed from a reflection of my face to show an image of a stone room. One of the castles in Nalhalla.

A small Mokian boy sat in front of the mirror. He grew alert the moment the image changed, then ran off, yelling. "Lord Smedry, Lord Smedry!"

Within seconds, my grandfather was there. He looked somewhat frazzled, his hair sticking out at odd angles, his bow tie on sideways. "Ah, Alcatraz, my lad! You did it!"

"I'm here, Grandpa," I said, nodding. "Inside Tuki Tuki. But things are bad here."

"Of course they are!" Grandpa said. "That's why we sent you in the first place, eh? Stay there for a moment. I need to get some knights!"

He rushed away. It looked like their half of the mirror had been hung on the wall in some kind of entryway or foyer.

I stood awkwardly for some time. The others crowded around me, looking through the mirror, waiting. Finally, Grandpa returned with several people dressed in full plate armor. One was Draulin, Bastille's mother. The other two were older-looking men.

"Alcatraz, tell them where you are," Grandpa Smedry said from somewhere to the side.

"I'm in Tuki Tuki," I said.

"You should leave there immediately," Draulin said sternly. "It is not safe, Lord Smedry."

"Yes, I know," I said. "But you know us Smedrys. Crazy, without any regard for our own safety!"

One of the knights frowned. "This does indeed offer the proof the elder Lord Smedry promised," he said.

"I sense we are being manipulated," the other said, shaking his head. "I do not like the feel of it."

Draulin remained quiet during the conversation. She seemed to be studying me carefully with those dark eyes of hers.

A thought occurred to me. They needed motivation to come help. Making a snap judgment, I turned the hand mirror around, shining it on Mallo. "Guess who's here with me?" I said to the knights.

Mallo looked shocked. "Alcatraz! What are you doing?"

"Trust me," I said.

"It's a Mokian warrior," one of the knights said. "I feel for his plight, but the rules of our order are—"

"Wait," Draulin's voice said suddenly. There was a silence, followed by her saying, "Your . . . Majesty?"

Mallo sighed visibly, shooting me a glare. "Yes, it is I."

"You are supposed to be safe!"

"I will not abandon my people," Mallo said.

I spun the mirror around. "So, it's not just a couple of foolish Smedrys, but the Mokian royal line who are in danger here. You should . . ."

The image in the glass started to grow turbulent, ripples moving through it. I frowned, shaking the mirror.

". . . can't . . . what . . . doing . . ." Draulin's voice said. "What . . . ?"

"I can't see you either," I said to them.

The others in the room crowded around. I lowered the mirror so all could see.

"That doesn't look good," Kaz said, rubbing his chin.

"This was supposed to last at least twenty days," Mallo said. "We—"

"General Mallo!" a voice cried. We turned as a young Mokian girl ran up the front steps to the palace and entered the main chamber.

"What is it?" Mallo asked, turning sharply.

"The Librarian army," the girl said. "They're doing something, something big. You should come see."

1010

Okay, I can't help myself. I've written three and a half books. I held my tongue. (Figuratively, unlike that guy back in Act V.) But I'm about to burst.

It is time to talk about religion in the Hushlands.

You Free Kingdomers may be confused by Hushlander religions. After all, they are all so very different, and their followers are all so very good at yelling at one another loudly that it's hard to tell what any of them are saying. However, should you infiltrate Librarian nations and need to imitate a Hushlander, you'll probably need to join one of their religions to blend in. Therefore, I've prepared this handy guide.

Religions, in the Hushlands, are basically about food.

That's right, food. In following one religion or another, you end up boycotting certain foods. If you become Hindu, for instance, you give up beef. Mormons give up alcohol and coffee. Catholics can eat pretty much whatever they want, but have to give up the stuff they like the most for one month a year, while Muslims give up *all* food during the daytime hours of Ramadan.

So which religion is the best? Well, it depends. In my cultivated opinion, I'd suggest Judaism.

But that's because I prefer the path of yeast resistance.

We stood atop the wooden palisade wall of Tuki Tuki watching the gigantic Librarian robots drive large, glowing rods into the ground. They shone blue in the night and were as tall as buildings. They illuminated the Librarian war camp, which was far more active now. Men and women had been awakened and were collecting their weapons and forming up in battle lines.

"What are they?" Angola asked.

"They look like some kind of glass device," Aydee said.

"No," Kaz said. He stood atop a stepstool and looked out at the Librarian camp, rubbing his chin. "This war is being led by the Order of the Shattered Lens."

"Who?" I asked.

Bastille rolled her eyes at my ignorance.

"The Shattered Lens is a Librarian sect, Al," Kaz said. He was a scholar of Talents, Oculatory distortions, and—by extension—Librarians. "You've met the Dark Oculators, the

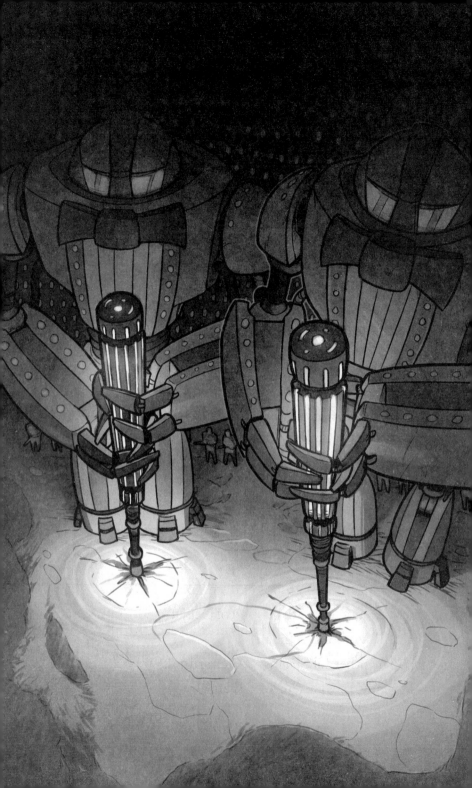

Scrivener's Bones, and the Wardens of the Standard. Well, the Shattered Lens is the last of them. And probably the largest. The other orders accept, even use, silimatic technology and Oculatory Lenses. These guys, though . . ."

"They don't?" I asked.

"They *hate* all forms of glass," Kaz said. "They take Biblioden's teachings very literally. He didn't like anything 'strange' like magic or silimatics. Most of the orders interpret his teachings as meaning 'Lenses and glasses need to be controlled *very* carefully, so only the important can use them.' Those Librarians hide the truth from most Hushlanders, but have no qualms about using Free Kingdomer technology and ideas when they can benefit from them.

"The Order of the Shattered Lens is different. *Very* different. They feel that Lenses and silimatic glasses should *never* be used, not even by Librarians. They think Free Kingdomer technology is evil and disgusting."

I nodded slowly. "So those piles of glass we passed while running into the city?"

"They hold glass-breakings," Angola said softly. "They gather together in groups and smash pieces of glass. Including regular glass, with no kind of Oculatory or silimatic abilities. It's symbolic to them."

"The other Librarians let them run the wars," Kaz added. "Partially, I suspect, to keep them away. There will be trouble within the Librarian ranks if the Free Kingdoms ever *do* fall. The Order of the Shattered Lens works with the Dark Oculators and the Scrivener's Bones for now. There's a bigger enemy to fight. But once we're gone, there will likely be civil war as the orders struggle for dominance."

"Civil war across the entire world," Bastille said softly, nodding. "The four Librarian sects using people as their pawns. The Shattered Lens trying to hunt down and kill Dark Oculators, the Wardens of the Standard trying to manipulate things with cool-headed politics, the Scrivener's Bones working for whoever will pay them the most . . ."

We fell silent. That army outside was large; I glanced back at the city. There didn't seem to be many Mokian soldiers. Perhaps five or six thousand, both men and women. The Librarians had easily four times that number, and they were armed with futuristic guns. The enormous robots continued their work, planting the rods in the ground. They were making a ring of them, encircling the city.

Faced by such daunting numbers, I finally began to realize what I'd gotten myself into. And that's when I invented the term *stoopidanated*, meaning "about as stoopid as Alcatraz Smedry, the day he snuck into Tuki Tuki just in time to be there when it got overwhelmed by Librarians."

It's a very specific word, I know. Odd how many times I've been able to use it in my life.

"So the rods aren't glass," I said. "What are they, then?"

"Plastic," Bastille guessed. "Some sort of glass-disrupting technology? That might be what's making the Communicator's Glass stop working."

"Might just be for light, though," Aydee said. "Look. Those rods are bright enough that the Librarians can move about as if it were day. They look like they're getting ready to attack." She shrank down a little bit on her stool, as if to hide behind the wall.

Something occurred to me. I pulled the Courier's Lenses out of my pocket and slid them on.

Now, it might seem odd to you Hushlanders that we had so many different ways of talking to one another over a distance. But if you think about it, this makes sense. How many different ways do we have in the Hushlands? Telephone, fax, telegraph, VoIP, e-mail, regular mail, radio, shouting really loud, bottles with notes in them, texting, blimps with advertisements on them, skywriting, voodoo boards, social media, smoke signals, etc.

Communicating with one another is a basic human need. And communicating with people far away is an even *more* basic human need, because that way we can make fun of people and they can't kick us in the face.

By the way, have I mentioned how ugly that shirt is? Yeah. Next time, please try to dress up a little bit when you read my books. Someone might see you, and I have a reputation to maintain.

I concentrated, feeding power into my Lenses, questing out for my grandfather. His face appeared in front of me, but it was fuzzy and indistinct.

Alcatraz, lad! Grandpa said. *I was hoping you'd use the Courier's Lenses. What's happening? Why doesn't the Communicator's Glass work?*

"I don't know," I replied. "The Librarians are doing something outside the city—planting these glowing rods in the ground. That might have something to do with it."

As I spoke, one of the robots placed another of the rods. When it did, my grandfather's form fuzzed even more.

"Grandfather," I said urgently. "Did we convince the knights?"

Think . . . enough . . . help . . . Grandfather said, his voice cutting in and out. *They know . . . king still . . . save His Majesty . . .*

"I can't understand you!" I said. Another robot raised a rod into the air, preparing to place it.

I raised my hands to the side of the glasses, focusing everything I had into the Lenses. I strained, teeth gritted. Shockingly, the glass started to glow, forcing me to close my eyes as they blazed alight. My grandfather's voice, once weak, surged back, audible again.

. . . Luring Lovecrafts, what a mess! I said I've nearly got

them persuaded. I'll bring them, lad, and anyone else I can get to come. We'll be there. Hold out until morning! Can you hear me, Alcatraz? Morning's first light. Er. Well, no, I'll be late. And that's been done before. But morning's second light, for certain. By third light at the latest. I promise!

The robot planted the rod. My grandfather's voice fuzzed again, and I tried another surge of power, but I'd pushed it too far. My Talent slipped through, mixing with my Oculatory power. I had trouble keeping the two separate; they were like two different colors of bright paint, mixing and churning inside of me. Use one, and some of the other always wanted to come along.

The Talent surged through my hands before I realized what I was doing, and the frames of the Lenses shattered. I caught the falling Lenses clumsily. Unfortunately, after feeling that resistance, I knew that they wouldn't work again—not as long as those Librarian rods were interfering. I reluctantly slipped the Lenses back in my pocket.

"What did he say?" Aydee asked, anxious.

"He's coming," I replied. "With the Knights of Crystallia."

"When?" Bastille asked.

"Well . . . he wasn't really that specific . . ." I grimaced. "He said dawn. Probably."

"Probably?" Mallo said. "Young Smedry, I'm not certain I can stake the lives of my people on a 'probably.'"

"My grandfather is reliable," I said. "He's never let me down."

"Except when he arrived too late to get the Sands of Rashid before the Librarians," Bastille added. "Or . . . well, when he arrived too late to stop your mother from stealing the Translator's Lenses from the Library of Alexandria. Or when he was too late to—"

"Thanks, Bastille," I said flatly. "Real helpful."

"I think we're all aware of my father's Talent," Kaz said, stepping up beside me. "But I know Leavenworth Smedry better than anyone else, now that Mom's dead. If my pop says he'll be here with help, you can count on him. He might be a tad late, but he'll make up for it with style."

"Style will not protect my people from Librarian weapons," Mallo said, shaking his head. "Your help is appreciated, but your promises are flimsy."

"Please," I said. "Your Majesty, you've *got* to give us a chance. At least give it until morning. What do you have to lose by sleeping on it?"

"There will be no sleeping," Mallo said, nodding. "Look."

I followed the gesture. Beyond the walls, the large robots had finished planting the rods into the ground. Now they were walking over to a large pile of boulders that sat just outside the camp.

"Our period of rest has ended," Mallo said grimly. "They

demanded our surrender, and since I've sent back no word, it seems they are going to resume their assaults. I had assumed they would wait until it was light to do so, but you know what they say about assumptions."

"If you're going to make a donkey joke," I noted, "I did that already."

Mallo frowned at me. "No, I was going to quote an ancient Mokian proverb, revered and honored by our people across six centuries of use."

"Oh," I said, embarrassed. "Um, sorry. How does it go?"

"'Don't make assumptions, idiot,'" Mallo quoted with a reverent voice.

"Nice proverb."

"Mokian philosophers like to get to the point," Mallo said. "Either way, if we are going to surrender, we need to do it now. Those terrible machines of theirs will begin throwing rocks soon, and the Shielder's Glass will not last much longer against the assault."

"If you give up," Bastille said, "that is the end of Mokia."

"Please," I said. "Give us more *time*. Wait just a little longer!"

"Husband," Angola said, laying a hand on his arm, "most of our people would rather die than be taken by the Librarians."

"Yes," Mallo said, "but sometimes you need to protect

people when they do not wish it. Our warriors think only of honor. But I must consider the future, and what is best for all of our people."

King Mallo's face adopted a thoughtful expression. He folded a pair of beefy arms, one of his soldiers holding his spear for him. He stared out over the top of the wooden wall, looking at the Librarian forces.

Now, perhaps some of you reading might be thinking of Mallo as a coward for *considering* surrender. That's great. Next time you're in charge of the lives of thousands of people, you can make decisions quickly if you want. But Mallo wanted to think.

It all comes back to change. Nothing stays the same, not even kingdoms. Sometimes you have to accept that.

Sometimes, though, things change too quickly for you to even think about it. What happened next is still a blur in my mind. We were standing on the wall, waiting for Mallo to make his decision. And then Librarians were there.

Apparently they came up through a tunnel they dug that opened just inside the wall. I didn't see that. I just saw a group of bow-tied figures charging at us along the wall, wielding guns that shot balls of light.

Kaz vanished, his Talent making him get Lost.

In the blink of an eye, three Mokian soldiers were standing in front of Aydee where there had been only two, her Talent instantly bringing a man from across the wall to defend her.

My Talent broke a few guns, though several of the Librarians had bows, and they fired those. Bastille, moving in a blur, had her sword out in a heartbeat and was cutting arrows from the air.

Seriously. She cut them *out of the air*. Never play baseball against a Crystin.

The Mokian soldiers began to fight, leveling their spears, which also shot out glowing bursts of light.

It was all over in a few seconds. I was the only one who didn't move. I had no training with real combat or war—I was just a stoopid kid who had gotten himself in over his head. By the time I thought to yelp in fear and duck, the skirmish was over, the assassins defeated.

Smoke rose in the air. Men fell still.

I glanced down, checking to make certain all of my important limbs were still attached. "Wow," I said.

Bastille stood in front of me, sword out, eyes narrow. She'd probably just saved my life.

"You see, Your Majesty," I said. "You can't trust the Librarians! If you give up, they will just . . ."

I trailed off, only then noticing something. Mallo wasn't

standing beside me, where he had been before. I searched around desperately, and found the king lying on the wall, his body covering that of his wife, whom he'd jumped to protect. Neither of them was moving.

Warriors called out in shock, moving to their king and queen. Others called for help. In a daze I turned, seeing the bodies of the Librarian assassins.

This was *actually* war. People were *actually* dying. Suddenly all of this didn't seem very funny any longer. Unfortunately, fate had a pretty good joke waiting for me in the very near future.

"They're alive," Bastille said, kneeling with the soldiers beside the king and queen. "They're still breathing. They don't look to have been hurt, even."

"The Librarian weapons," one of the Mokians said, "will often knock people unconscious. They're trying to conquer Mokia but don't want to exterminate us. They want to rule over us. So they use guns that put us into comas."

Another of the men nodded. "We know of no cure—our stunner blasts work differently and have their own antidote. Those wounded can only be awakened by the Librarians, once the war is over. They'll wake us up in small, controllable batches, and brainwash us to forget our freedom."

"I've heard of this," Kaz said, kneeling down beside the king. When had Kaz come back? "They did it when conquering other kingdoms too. Brutally effective tactic—if they knock us into comas, we still have to feed and care for our wounded, which drains our resources. Makes it easier to crack us. Far more effective than just killing."

One of the soldiers nodded. "We have thousands of wounded who are sleeping like this. Of course, many of the Librarians lie comatose from our stun-spears as well. The antidote for one does not work on victims of the other."

We stood back as a Mokian doctor approached. Surprisingly, he was dressed in a white lab coat and spectacles. He carried a large piece of glass, which he held up, using it to inspect the king and queen. "No internal wounds. Just Librarian Sleep."

"I would have expected a witch doctor," I said quietly to Kaz.

"Why?" Kaz said. "The king's not a witch, and neither's the queen."

"Take them to their chambers," the doctor said, standing. "And place double guards on them! If the Librarians know they're down, they'll want to kidnap them."

Several soldiers nodded. Others, however, stood up, looking around with confusion. Outside, the Librarian robots began to hurl their boulders. One smashed against the glass dome, making the entire city seem to shake.

"Who is in charge now?" I asked, looking around.

"The captain of the watch fell earlier today," one of the soldiers said. "And the last remaining field general before him."

"The princess rules," another said.

"But she's outside the city."

"The Council of Kings will need to ratify a succession," another said. "There's no official king until then. Acting king would be highest person of peerage in the city."

The group fell silent.

"Which means?" I asked.

"By the Spire itself," Bastille whispered, eyes opening wide. "It can't be. No . . ."

All eyes turned toward me.

"Wait," I said, nervous. "What?"

"The Smedry Clan is peerage," Bastille said, "accepted as lords and ladies in all nations belonging to the Council of Kings. Your family gained that right when they abdicated; all recognized that the Smedry Talents could have led you to conquer the Free Kingdoms. But because of that, a direct heir to the Smedry line ranks equal with a duke in most kingdoms. Including Nalhalla and Mokia."

"And a duke is . . . ?" I asked.

"Just under a prince," Aydee said.

The warriors all fell to one knee before me. "What are your wishes, Your Majesty?" one of them said.

"Aw, *pelicans*," Kaz swore.

Chapter
24601

Many of you in the Free Kingdoms have heard about the day I was crowned king of Mokia. It's become quite the legend. And legends have a habit of being exaggerated.

In a way, a legend is like an organism—a virus or a bacteria. It begins as a fledgling story, incubating in just a couple of people. It grows as it is passed to others, and they give it strength. Mutating it. Enlarging it. It grows grander and grander, infecting more and more of the population, until it becomes an epidemic.

The only cure for a legend is pure, antiseptic truth. That's partially why I began writing these books. How did I end up leading Mokia? Well, I was never really king—just "acting monarch" as they put it. I was the highest-ranked person in the town, but only because most everyone else had either fallen or been sent away.

So no, I didn't heroically take up the king's sword in the middle of battle, as the legend says. My ascent to the throne was not announced by angelic voices. Very little heroism was involved.

But there *was* a whole lot of confusion.

"*What*?" I demanded. "I can't be king! I'm only thirteen years old!"

"You're not our king, my lord," one of the Mokians said. "Just our acting monarch."

Another rock boomed against the city's dome. Spiderweb cracks formed up the side of the glass.

"Well, what do I do?" I asked, glancing at Kaz, Aydee, and Bastille for support.

"Someone has to make the decision for us, my lord," said one of the Mokian soldiers. "The king was about to surrender. Do we go through with it, or do we fight?"

"You're going to make *me* decide?"

They just kept kneeling around me, waiting.

I looked over my shoulder, toward the Librarian camp. The sky was black, but the area around the city was lit as if by floodlights. I could see several places where the Librarians were digging tunnels, using some kind of strange, rodlike

devices that appeared to vibrate the dirt and make it move away. The robots kept throwing rocks against the dome.

BOOM! BOOM! BOOM!

Just moments before, I'd been incredulous that the king would consider surrender. But now the same question fell on me, and it terrified me. I had just seen people die. Librarian soldiers who had come to kill—or at least incapacitate—the king. Could I send the Mokian warriors to perhaps suffer the same fate?

Talk of bravery and freedom was one thing. But it felt different to be the one who made the decision. If I gave the order, the men and women who got hurt, killed, or knocked out would be *my* responsibility. That was a lot to heap on the shoulders of a thirteen-year-old kid who hadn't even *known* about Mokia six months ago. And people wonder why I'm so screwed up.

"We fight," I said quietly.

This seemed to be the answer the soldiers were waiting for. They yelped in excitement, raising their spears—which, as I'd just learned, could shoot a stunning blast like the Librarian guns.

"You," I said, picking the Mokian who'd been doing the talking. He was a lanky fellow with a lot of war paint and his black hair in a buzz cut. "What's your name?"

"Aluki," he said proudly. "Sergeant of the wall guard."

"Well, you're now acting as my second in command." I glanced at the sky, cringing as another rock hit the dome. Above, the moon shone full and bright. The same moon that shone on the Hushlands. "What time is it? How long until dawn?"

"It's not even eleven yet," Kaz said, checking his pocket watch. "Seven hours, maybe?"

"Spread the word," I said to the soldiers on the wall around me. "We have to survive for only *seven hours*. Help will come after that."

They nodded, running off to pass the word. Aluki stayed nearby. I turned to the side; Bastille was regarding me with folded arms. I cringed, waiting for her to scour me with condemnations for being so arrogant as to let the Mokians make me king.

"We'll need to do something about those tunnels," she said. "We won't hold out for long if teams keep slipping into the city like that."

"Huh?" I asked.

"Don't forget the robots," Kaz said as a rock hit above. "Woodpeckers! That glass is close to cracking. If the dome falls, the tunnels will be our *last* concern."

"True," Bastille said. "Maybe we could do something about the fallen troops, the ones in comas. If we could get them to wake up somehow . . ."

"Wait!" I said, looking back and forth between the two. "Aren't you going to state the obvious?"

"What?" Bastille said. "That the Shattered Lens has far better technology than we thought?" She narrowed her eyes in a very Bastille-like way, glancing at the enormous machines that were tossing rocks toward the city. She seemed to have a particular dislike for them, along the lines of her hatred of walls. (Read book one.)

"No," I said, exasperated. "That I have no business being king! I can barely lead myself to the bathroom in the morning, let alone command an entire army."

"Too late to change that now, Al," Kaz said with a shrug.

"I think you'll do a great job," Aydee added. "Being king isn't that tough, from what I hear. Use a lot of phrases like 'you please the crown' or 'we are not amused' and occasionally make up a holiday."

"Yeah," I said flatly. "Sounds as easy as one plus one."

"Seven?" Aydee asked, cocking her head.

I looked at Bastille. She still had her arms folded. "Kaz, Aydee," she said, "why don't you go get a count and see how many troops we have? Also, Alcatraz will need to know what kind of shape the command structure is in."

The two Smedrys nodded, hurrying off to do as requested.

"Wait!" Bastille said, turning with a sudden shock. "Kaz,

you do the counting. Aydee, you stay away from anything of the sort."

"Good call," Kaz said.

"Right!" Aydee called. "I'll give moral support."

And they left. That, unfortunately, meant I was now alone on the wall with Bastille. I gulped, backing away as she walked toward me. My back eventually hit the wall behind; if I retreated any farther, I'd topple over and fall to my death on the ground outside the city.

I considered it anyway.

Bastille reached me, placing a finger against my chest. "You," she said, "are *not* going to fail these people."

"But—"

"I'm tired of you wavering back and forth, Alcatraz," she said. "Shattering Glass! Half the time, you act like you're panicked by the idea of being in charge, then the other half the time you just take control!"

"I . . . er . . . well . . ."

"And the other half the time you babble incoherently!"

"I like babbling!" I exclaimed. (I'm not sure why.) "Besides, that sounds like some Aydee math. Three halves?"

She eyed me.

"Yes, you're right about me," I said. "Sometimes this all feels like a game. It twists my head in knots to think of the things I've been through, the things that have become part of my life. I get carried away with it all, with what everyone expects of me just because of my name.

"But I've already decided I want to lead. I decided it months ago. I want to be a hero; I want to be a leader. But that doesn't mean I want to be a *king*! When I stop to think about it, I realize how insane it is."

"Then don't stop to think," Bastille said. "I don't see why it should be so hard. Not thinking seems to be one of your specialties."

I grimaced. "The things you say to me don't help either, Bastille. Every time I think that I'm starting to do well, I get a face-full of insults from you. And I can never tell if I deserve them or not!"

She narrowed her eyes farther, finger pressed against my sternum. I cringed, preparing for the storm.

"I like you," she said.

I blinked, righting myself. "What?"

"I. Like. You. So I insult you."

I scratched at my head. ".drawkcab ecnetnes a epyt ot dluow ti sa esnes hcum sa tuoba sekam taht ,ellitsaB"

She scowled at me, lowering her hand. "If you don't understand, I'm not going to explain it to you."

Boys, welcome to the wonderful world of talking to women about their feelings. As a handy primer, here are a few things you should know:

1. Women have feelings.
2. You will spend the next seventy years or so trying to guess what they're feeling and why.
3. You will be wrong most of the time.
4. I like french fries.

That's about all the help I can give you, I'm afraid. If it's any consolation, at least the women in *your* life don't have anger-management issues and a tendency to carry around five-foot-long magical swords.

"Look," Bastille said. "It's not important. What's important is saving Mokia. If you didn't notice, that was my *sister* who just got towed away unconscious. I'm not going to let the kingdom fall while she's out."

"But shouldn't a Mokian be king?"

"You are Mokian," Bastille said. "And Nalhallan, and Fracois, and Unkulu. You're a Smedry—you're considered a citizen of all kingdoms. Besides, you *do* have Mokian blood in you. The Smedry line and the Mokian royal line has often intermixed. It wasn't odd for your uncle Millhaven to marry a Mokian. His wife is a third cousin of Mallo's, and your great-great-grandfather was the son of a Mokian prince."

I blinked. Bastille, it should be noted, rarely shows her princessly nature. She has a tendency to rip up anything pink, her singing sounds remarkably like the sound produced when you drop a rock on the tail of a wildebeest, and the last time a sweet flock of forest animals showed up and tried to help her clean, she chased them for the better part of an hour, swinging her sword and cursing like a sailor.

But she *does* think like a king's daughter sometimes. And she was force-fed all kinds of princessly information as a child, including long, boring lists of royal family trees. She knows which prince married which hypercountess and which superduke is cousins with which earl.

Yes. In the Free Kingdoms, we have royal titles like superdukes and hypercountesses. It's complicated.

"So . . . I really *am* in the royal line," I said, shocked.

"Of course you are. You're a Smedry—you're related to three quarters of the kings and queens out there."

"But not you, right?"

"What? No. Not in any important way. We might be fourteenth, upside-down ubercousins or something."

I eyed her, trying to figure out what the gak an "upside-down ubercousin" was. Sounded like the kind of drink a kid my age wasn't allowed to order.

It should be noted that Bastille and I are certainly *not* directly related. At least, we weren't at that point.

"All right," I said. "But I don't know anything about running a war."

"Fortunately, I do. Troop morale and logistics were part of

my training as a princess, and I have practice with battlefield tactics as part of my Crystin training."

"Great! You can take over for me, then!"

She shook her head, eyes going wide, face getting a little white. "Don't be stoopid."

"Er, why not?"

As I think about it, that was kind of a stoopid answer, which was fitting, if you think about it. Me, I try not to think about anything. Oooh . . . shiny . . .

Bastille grimaced. "You need to ask? I'm not what these people need. I'm not inspiring. *You* are. You're a king. I'm a general. They're different, with different sets of skills." She nodded toward the Mokian soldiers standing atop the walls. A lot of them didn't look much like warriors. Oh, they had war paint and spears. But not many of them were muscular.

"Mokia is a kingdom of scholars and craftspeople, Alcatraz," Bastille said softly. "Why do you think the Librarians attacked here first? They've been besieged for months now, their country at war for years. Many of the trained soldiers have already been knocked unconscious or killed. Do you have any idea what the loss of both the king and queen could mean? They're demoralized, wounded, and beaten down."

She lifted her finger, tapping me in the chest again. "They need someone to lead them. They need someone *spectacular*, someone miraculous. Someone who can keep them fighting for just a little longer, until your grandfather arrives with help."

"And, uh, that someone is me?"

"Yes," she said, almost grudgingly. "I told you a few months back that I believed in you. Well, I do. I believe in what you can be when you're confident. Not when you're *arrogant*, but when you're confident. When you decide to do something, really decide, you do amazing things. I wish you could be that person a little more often."

I scratched my head. "I think that person is a lie, Bastille. I'm not confident. I just get lucky."

"You get lucky a lot. Particularly when we really need it. You saved your father, you got the Sands back, you rescued the monarchs."

"That last one was mostly you," I said with a grimace.

"The idea that got us free was yours," she said, "and you spotted Archedis."

I shrugged. "It seems that when I get desperate, my mind works better. I'm not sure if that's something to be proud of or not."

"Well, it's what we've got," Bastille said, "so we're going to work with it. I'll organize the troops. *You* be confident, give the Mokians the sense that someone's in charge. We'll hold this city together until the Old Smedry gets here."

"He'll probably be late, you know."

"Oh, I'm certain he will be," Bastille said. "The question isn't, 'Will he be late?' The question is, 'How late is he going to be?'"

I nodded grimly.

"You ready to be a king?" she asked.

I hesitated just briefly. "Yes."

"Good," she said, spinning as screams erupted from the center of the city. "Because I think another group of Librarians just tunneled in."

Chapter
° 070706 °

Don't yawn.

I shouldn't have agreed to be king. If you've been following these books, you know that my early experiences set me up to fail. Being a celebrity made me think that I was much more important than I really was, and success led me to take more responsibility than I should have. That all meant when I did fall, I fell really far.

You yawning yet? No? Good. You most definitely *don't* want to part your lips, suck in that sweet air, and feel the relaxing release as you stretch and let your mouth open wide. You itch to do it; you've been reading for a while now, and you're getting a little groggy. But don't yawn. Really, don't do it.

Accepting the crown of Mokia, if even for a short time,

was the culminating peak of my spiral to fame. The events of this siege became infamous. In fact, I didn't realize what I'd done until long afterward. (After leaving Mokia, after all, I returned to the Hushlands.)

Some Hushlanders think we yawn to increase oxygen to the brain, but researchers have recently discounted that theory. They're right to do so. In the Free Kingdoms, it's been known for a long time that yawns frighten away bloogynaughts. You know what bloogynaughts are, don't you? They're those things that sneak up on people while they're reading books, lurking just behind them, watching them, edging closer and closer until they're right there. Behind you. Breathing on your neck. About ready to grab you. A yawn would scare it away. If only you could yawn . . .

Why did I agree to be king? I should have said no. And yet I didn't. I let them make me king. I let Bastille persuade me. I let them set me up high.

Why? Well, perhaps for the same reason that—when reading the paragraphs above—you had a powerful urge to yawn or glance over your shoulder. Talk about something long enough, and people will start thinking about it. It's kind of like a twisted, funky kind of mind control. Bastille was a princess, my family had once held thrones, and I was related distantly to pretty much every monarch in the Free Kingdoms. I guess I wanted to feel what it was like to be king.

(In the end, I discovered that being a king feels pretty much like being a regular person, only people shoot at you more often.)

Bastille and I charged through the city, racing toward the screams. Mokian men and women threw down the things they had been working on and rallied to the breach. Bastille slipped her sunglasses on, and I nodded to her. She took off at a much faster speed, leaving me behind as she used her enhanced Crystin speed to dart toward the disturbance.

I ran much more slowly, but I made a fair showing of it. The last half a year or so had been very good for my constitution. If you want to practice for a footrace, I'd highly recommend the Alcatraz Smedry training regimen. It involves being chased by Librarians, half-metal monsters, evil apparitions, sentient romance novels, fallen Knights of Crystallia, and the occasional evil chicken named Moe. Our success rate in training footrace winners is ninety-five percent. Unfortunately, our survival rate is about five percent, so it kind of balances everything out.

A group of Mokians filled in around me, running at my same speed. At first I thought they were joining me to rush to the scene of the disturbance. However, they were keeping too close. I realized with shock that they were an honor guard, of the type that run around protecting kings and saying, "Who dares disturb the king?" and stuff like that. That made me feel important.

Even running as fast as we could, we arrived too late to help with the fighting. The Librarians had come out of a large, gopher-hole-like pit in the ground of a wide green field near what I'd later learn was Mokian Royal University. Some bodies lay on the ground, and it made my stomach twist to see how many were Mokian. At least they weren't dead. Of course, being in a coma was worse in many ways.

You may be shocked at how "civilized" war is out in the Free Kingdoms. However, realize that they do what they do for a reason. If the Librarians could capture Tuki Tuki, they could get the antidote for the sleeping sickness—and they'd get nearly their entire army back to keep fighting, moving inward, to conquer more of the Free Kingdoms. It made sense for the Librarians to encourage the use of the coma guns and coma spears.

This latest group of Librarian infiltrators, strangely, looked like they'd surrendered soon after climbing out of the hole. Why hadn't they fought longer? They stood with their hands up, surrounded by ragged Mokian fighters. Bastille watched nearby, arms folded, looking dissatisfied. Likely because she hadn't gotten a chance to stab anyone.

The Mokians should have been happy to have won the skirmish so easily. But most of them just looked exhausted. The field was lit by torches on long poles rammed into the ground, and boulders still struck the dome protecting the city. Each one seemed to crack it a little bit more.

"We can't hold out!" said one of the spear-wielding Mokians. "Look! They know they can surrender if we rally to fight them. There are so many of them that they're content to lose an entire team to knock out a few of us."

"It's probably a distraction," another soldier said. "They're digging in other places too."

"They're going to overrun us."

"We've lost."

"We—"

"Stop!" Bastille bellowed, waving her arms and getting their attention. "*Stop being stupid!*" She folded her arms, as if that was all she intended to say. Which, knowing Bastille, might just be the case.

"We *haven't* lost," I said, stepping forward. "We can win. We just need to hold out a little longer."

"We can't!" one of the soldiers said. "There are only a few thousand of us left. There aren't enough people to patrol the streets to look for tunnelers. Most of us have been awake for three days straight!"

"And so you'd give up?" I demanded, looking at them. "That's how they win. By making us give up. I've *lived* in Librarian lands. They don't win because they conquer, they win because they make people stop caring, stop wondering.

They'll tire you out, then feed you lies until you start repeating them, if only because it's too hard to keep arguing."

I looked around at the men and women in their islander wraps, holding spears that burned. They seemed ashamed. The field was shockingly quiet; even the captive Librarians didn't say anything.

"This is how they win," I repeated. "They *need* you to give in. They *have to* make you stop fighting. They don't rule the Hushlands with chains, fire, and oppression. They rule it with comfort, leisure, and easy lies. It's easy to accept the normal and avoid thinking about the difficult and the strange. Life can be so much simpler if you stop dreaming.

"But *that* is how we defeat them. They can never win, so long as we refuse to believe in their lies. Even if they take Tuki Tuki, even if Mokia falls, even if *all* of the Free Kingdoms become theirs. They will never win so long as we refuse to believe. Don't give up, and you will not lose. I promise you that."

Around me, the Mokians began to nod. Several smiled, holding their spears more certainly.

"But what will we do?" a female warrior asked. "How will we survive?"

"My grandfather is coming," I said. "We just have to last a little longer. I'll talk to my counselors . . ." I hesitated. "Er, I have counselors, don't I?"

"We're right here, Your Majesty," a voice said. I glanced backward, to where three Mokians stood in official-looking wraps, wearing small, colorful caps on their heads. I vaguely remembered them joining me as I ran toward the disturbance.

"Great," I said. "I'll talk to my counselors, and we'll figure something out. You soldiers, your job is to keep *hoping*. Don't give up. Don't let them win your hearts, even if they look like they'll win the city."

Looking back on that speech, it seems incredibly stoopi-dalicious. Their kingdom was about to fall, their king and queen were casualties, and what was I telling them? "Just keep believing!" Sounds like the title of a cheesy '80s rock ballad.

People believe in themselves all the time yet still fail. Wanting something badly enough doesn't really change anything, otherwise I'd be a popsicle. (Read book one.)

Yet in this case, my advice was oddly accurate. The Librar-ians have always preferred to rule in secret. Biblioden taught that to enslave someone, you were best off making them comfortable. Mokia couldn't fall, not completely, unless the Mokians allowed themselves to be turned into Hush-landers.

Sounds impossible, right? Who would *let* themselves be turned into Hushlanders? Well, you didn't see how tired the Mokians were, how much the extended war had beaten them down. It occurred to me at that moment that maybe the

Librarians could have won months ago. They'd kept on fighting precisely because they knew they didn't just have to win, they had to *overwhelm*. Kind of how you might keep playing a video game against your little brother, even though you know you can win at any moment, because you're planning the biggest, most awesome, most *crushing* combo move ever.

Except the Librarians were doing it with the hearts of the people of Mokia. And that made me angry.

The soldiers rushed off to get back to their other duties. I eyed the Librarian captives. Had they surrendered too easily? The Mokians didn't seem terribly threatening. Perhaps Bastille had surprised them; facing a bunch of soldiers who hadn't slept in days was one thing, but a fully trained Crystin was another.

I turned to my advisers. There were three of them, two men and a woman. The first man was tall and thin, with a long neck and spindly arms. He was kind of shaped like a soda bottle. The woman next to him was shorter and had a compact look to her, arms pulled in at her sides, hunched over, chin nestled down level with her shoulders. She looked kind of like a can of soda. The final man was large, wide, and thick-bodied. He was husky, with a small head, and kind of looked like . . . well, a large two-liter soda bottle.

"Someone get me something to drink," I barked to my

honor guard, then walked up to the soda-pop triplets. "You're my advisers?"

"We are," said soda-can woman. "I'm Mink, the large fellow to my left is Dink, and the man to my right is Wink."

"Mink, Dink, and Wink," I said, voice flat. (Like soda that's been left out too long.)

"No relation," Dink added.

"Thanks for clearing that up," I said. "All right, advise me."

"We should give up," Dink said.

"Good speech," Mink added, "but it sounded too much like a rock ballad."

"That jacket looks good on you," Wink said.

"Er, thank you, Wink," I said, confused.

"Oh, Wink got caught in an unfortunate Librarian dishar-
mony grenade," Mink added. "Messed up his brain a little bit.
He gives great advice . . . it's just not always on the topic you
want at the moment."

"Never get involved in a land war in Asia," Wink added.

"Great," I said. "So you think there's no way out of this?"

"The dome is going to crack soon," Dink said, shaking his
head.

"These burrows are coming more frequently," Mink said.
"They'll keep digging into our city, knocking more and more
people into comas until there's nobody left to fight back."

"Always wear a hat when feeding pigeons," Wink added.

All three of us looked at him. Wink shrugged. "Think
about it for a moment. You'll figure out why."

"So," Bastille said, walking up, arms folded, "you're saying
that if we can keep the dome from falling and protect against
the people digging in, we can hold out."

The three advisers looked at one another. "I guess," Mink
said. "But how are you going to do *that*?"

"Alcatraz will figure something out," Bastille said.

"I will?"

"You'd better."

"Never trust a three-fingered lion tamer."

"Why are you so sure I'll figure something out?"

"Because that's what you *do*."

"And if I can't this time?"

"If you run out of toothpaste, you can make your own by mixing two parts baking soda with one part salt and some water."

"I just said that you would."

"Well, I'll bet it would help if we could destroy those robots."

"How?"

"An onion a day keeps *everyone* away."

"Teddy bears! We could use those purple bear grenades, the type that destroy nonliving things."

"We don't have enough of them."

"Don't the Mokians have any?"

"I checked. They used all of theirs."

"Always throw paper first."

"Hey, guys! What are you doing?"

"Aydee, Alcatraz is going to come up with a brilliant plan to stop the robots."

"Cool!"

"You're always so bubbly."

"Kind of like soda pop."

"Someone needs to get you a drink, Alcatraz."

"I know."

"Boom!"

"Did you just say, 'Boom,' Alcatraz?"

"No, that was the rock hitting the ceiling. We *really* need to stop those!"

"Arr!"

"Wait, what?"

"It's me, Kaz. I was going to say, 'Are you guys done jabbering yet?' But I stubbed my toe."

"Arr!"

"Kaz!"

"That time it wasn't me. It was sexybeard the pirate."

"Hey, guys. Arr."

"Whatever."

"Fool me once, shame on you. Fool me twice, shame on me. Fool me three times, and I'll hire you as my lawyer."

"Wait, I'm lost."

"That's not surprising for you, Kaz."

"Who's talking?"

"I am."

"Who are you?"

"Aluki."

"When did *you* get here?"

"Oh, a page back or so. Looked like a real dangerous conversation to get into."

"Alcatraz, the rocks! We have to stop them."

"We need more teddy bears. Wow. Never thought I'd ever use *that* sentence."

"Nobody *has* more bears."

"Yes . . . but I just thought of something to fix that."

"Should I be scared?"

"Probably."

"Always remember, foursight is what Oculators have when wearing their Lenses."

"Shiver me timbers!"

"All right, Aydee. I've got a question for you. It's going to be a hard one. The hardest math problem you've ever seen."

"Er . . . I don't know . . ."

"Alcatraz, are you sure you want to do this?"

"No."

"Great. That's comforting."

"It's the best thing I've got right now. Aydee, I'm going to ask you a math question, and I want you to keep the number in your head. Only spit it out when we get done, all right?"

"Okay . . ."

"Take one and add fourteen."

"Er . . ."

"Then take away nine."

"Right."

"Then multiply by seventy-four."

"Um . . ."

"Then subtract three."

"Well . . ."

"Then take the square root of that."

"What's a square root?"

"Then take one third of that."

"Got it."

"Then multiply by negative one."

"Okay."

"*What*?"

"Hush, Bastille. Then add the number of inches in a foot."

"That's easy."

"It is? I'm lost."

"Quiet, Kaz. Then add eleven billion."

"Okay . . ."

"Then subtract eleven and one billion."

"This is getting hard."

"Then take the square root of that."

"Oh, I remember! A square root is a carrot that doesn't know how to dance, right?"

"Batten down the hatches!"

"Then subtract one. That's *exactly* the number of purple bear grenades we have left. How many have we got, Aydee?"

"Uh . . . er . . . um . . ."

"I think her brain is going to explode, Al."

"Hush. You can do it, Aydee. I know you can."

"I . . . carry the one . . . multiply by *i*. Take the complex derivative of Avogadro's number . . . I've got it, Alcatraz! Five thousand, three hundred and fifty-seven. Wow! I didn't know we had that many bears!"

Kaz, Bastille, and I glanced at each other. Then we looked at Kaz's pack, which held the bears. He took it off in a flash, hurling it away.

He was just fast enough. The pack ripped apart and a mountain of teddy bears burst free—5,357 of them, to be precise. They flooded out, piling on top of one another, making a mountain of purple exploding teddy bears as large as a building.

"Aydee, you're amazing," I said.

"Thanks! I think I'm getting better at math. I hope it doesn't ruin my Talent."

"I think you're fine," Bastille said dryly, picking herself up off the ground from where she'd ducked, anticipating the explosion of teddy bears.

"That's a big ol' mound of bears," Kaz said, folding his arms. "I think it's time to hunt us some robots."

"Be careful, Your Majesty," Wink warned. "Some robots are unbearable."

"Your Majesty," Mink said, brushing off her wrap. "Perhaps you should decide what to do with the prisoners first."

I glanced to the side. The guards were still standing there, watching over the group of suit-, skirt-, and bow-tie-wearing Librarians. The Mokians looked very anxious. The Librarians seemed bored.

"Do we have a dungeon or something?" I asked. "We should..." I trailed off, noticing something odd. Frowning, I stepped forward. One of the captive Librarians, huddled near the middle, was hiding her face, looking pointedly away from me. She had blonde hair and angular features. As she tried to stay hidden, I caught her eyes and recognized them for certain.

"*Mother?*" I asked, shocked.

Chapter

$$6.022140857 \times 10^{23}$$

Are you surprised? My mother showed up completely unexpectedly in Tuki Tuki when I just happened to be there fighting? How unforeseeable!

What? You're not surprised? Why not? Is it because my mother has unexpectedly shown up in *every single one of these books so far*? (It's a mathematical law: One point is a point, two points a line, three points a plane, four points a cliché. I think Archimedes discovered it first.)

This plays into one of the big problems for writers. You see, we tend to skip the boring parts. If we didn't, our novels would be filled of sections like this one:

I got up in the morning and brushed my teeth, then went to the bathroom and took a shower. Nothing exciting happened. I ate breakfast. Nothing exciting happened. I went out

to get the newspaper. I saw a squirrel. It wasn't very exciting. Then I came in and watched cartoons. They were boring.
I scratched my armpit. Then I went to the bathroom again.
Then I took a nap. My evil Librarian mother did not show up
and harass me. That evening, I clipped my toenails. Yippee.

* * *

See? You're asleep now, aren't you? That was mind-numb-
ingly, excruciatingly boring. In fact, you're not even reading
this, are you? You're dozing. I could make fun of your stoopid
ears and you would never know.

HEY YOU! WAKE UP!

There. You back? Good. Anyway, we don't include all of that
stuff because it tends to put people to sleep. I spent months
between books three and four doing pretty much nothing
other than going to the bathroom and scratching my armpits.

I tend to write about the exciting stuff. (This introduction
excepted. Sorry.) And that's the stuff that my mother tends to
be part of. So it's hard to keep it surprising when she shows
up, since every section I write about tends to be one where she
gets involved.

So let's start this again. This time, do me the favor of at
least *pretending* to be surprised. Maybe hit your head with the

book a few times to daze yourself. That'll make it easier for you to exclaim in surprise when she shows up. (Remember, you should be acting this all out.)

Ahem.

"*Mother?*" I asked, shocked.

"Hello, Alcatraz," the woman said, sighing. Shasta Smedry—also known as Ms. Fletcher—wore a sharp business suit and had her hair in a bun. She wore thin, horn-rimmed spectacles, though she wasn't an Oculator. Her face had a pinched look to it, as if she were perpetually smelling something unpleasant.

"What are you *doing* here?" I demanded, stepping up to the Mokian guards, who stood in a ring around the Librarians. I didn't get too close. My mother isn't the safest person to be around.

"Really, Alcatraz, I would have thought you'd be more observant. What am I doing? Obviously I'm helping to conquer this meaningless, insignificant city."

I eyed her, and her image *wavered* slightly. I was shocked by that, but I was currently wearing my Oculator's Lenses. They read auras of things with Oculatory power, but they could do other strange things. Things like give me a nudge to notice something I should have seen.

In this case, I realized what I should do. I took the Oculator's Lenses off and tucked them away. Then I got out my single Truthfinder's Lens, which was suspended in a set of spectacles that was missing the other lens. I slipped this on, smiling at my mother.

She shut her mouth, looking dissatisfied. She knew what that Lens was. She wouldn't be able to lie, at least not without me spotting it.

"Let me repeat the question," I said. "What are you doing here?"

My mother folded her arms. Unfortunately, there was an easy way to defeat the Truthfinder's Lens: by not talking. But fortunately, keeping my mother from saying snide remarks is like keeping me from saying stoopid ones: theoretically possible, but never observed in the wild.

"You're a fool," Shasta finally said. Puffs of white smoke came from her mouth, visible only to my single Truthfinder-covered eye. She was telling the truth—or at least what she saw as the truth. "This city is doomed." More white. "Why did you come here, Alcatraz? You should have stayed safe in Nalhalla."

"Safe? In a city where you kidnapped me and nearly let your Librarian allies slaughter my friends?"

"That was unfortunate," Shasta said. "I didn't wish for it to happen." All true, surprisingly.

"You let it happen anyway. And now you've followed me here. Why?"

"I didn't follow you here," she snapped. "I—" she cut off, as if realizing she'd said too much.

She stopped as I smiled. The first statement had been true. She *wasn't* there because of me. She'd come for other reasons. But why? I doubted it was simply because she wanted to see Tuki Tuki captured. When my mother was involved, things were always a whole lot deeper than they seemed.

"Have you seen my father?" I asked.

She looked away, obviously determined not to say anything. Above, the rocks kept beating against the dome. A chunk of glass broke free, tumbling down to the city a short distance away. I could hear it shatter, like a thousand icicles falling off a rooftop at once.

There wasn't time to chat with my mother right now. "Throw them in my dungeons," I said to Aluki. "I . . . er, I do have dungeons, don't I?"

"Not really," Aluki said. "We've been keeping prisoners in the university catacombs. They have Reinforcer's Glass in the walls, which would make it almost impossible for the Librarians to tunnel in and rescue them."

"Very well. Throw them in the university basement and lock them away," I said. I pointed at my mother. "Except her. Lock her someplace *extra* safe. And search her. She stole a book from Nalhalla that we will want to recover."

"I don't have that anymore," Shasta said. Unfortunately,

the Lens said she was telling the truth. She was also smiling slyly, as if she knew something important.

She couldn't have read it, I thought. *Not without a pair of Translator's Lenses. And she didn't come here to get my pair; she didn't know I would be here.*

The soldiers led Shasta and the other Librarians away. As they did, I noticed one of them watching me. He was an older man and didn't look anything like a soldier. He wore a tuxedolike suit with a cravat at the neck, and he had a short, graying beard flecked with black. He had keen, sagacious eyes.

"Search that one too," I said, grabbing Aluki's arm and pointing the man out. "I don't like how he looked at me."

"Yes, Your Majesty," Aluki said.

"You don't like how he 'looked' at you?" Bastille asked, walking up to me.

"There's something about him," I said. "He's odd. I mean, the only reason to wear a cravat is to look distinguished and intriguing. It's kind of like using "sagacious" in a sentence; it's less about what it actually means, and more about making you look smart."

Bastille frowned, but Kaz nodded as if understanding. Aydee had run over to the bears and was gleefully counting them out into piles of ten. She gave each one a hug and a name before setting it aside. It was kind of cute, if you ignored the fact that each and every one of those bears was a live grenade.

My three counselors stood, speaking quietly next to the large pile of bears.

Bastille followed my gaze. "That was dangerous, what you did, Smedry."

"What? Multiplying the bears?" I shrugged. "It could have gone the other direction, I suppose, and Aydee's Talent could have made our stock vanish. But I figured that we only had a few bears left, and that wasn't enough to do what we needed to. So what did we have to lose?"

"I'm not worried about what we could have lost," Bastille said. "I'm worried about what we could have *gained*."

"Wait? Huh?" (You say stuff like that a lot when you're as dumb as I am.)

"Shattering Glass, Smedry! What would have happened if Aydee had said we had fifty thousand bears? What if she'd said four or five *million* bears! We'd have been buried in them. You could have destroyed the city, smothering everyone inside of it."

I cringed, an image popping into my head of purple teddy bears washing over the city. Of the Mokians being crushed beneath the weight of a sea of pleasant plushness. A tsunami of teddies doing the Librarians' work for them. A blitzkrieg of bears, a torrent of toys, an . . . um . . . upheaval of ursines.

Or, in simpler terms, a *shattering* lot of bears.

"Gak!" I said.

"That's right," Bastille said. She wagged a finger at me. "Smedry Talents are dangerous, particularly in the young. I'd have thought that you—of all people—would realize this."

"Oh, don't be such a bubble in the glass, Bastille," Kaz said, smacking me on the arm. "You did great, kid. That kind of bear firepower is *just* the type of thing Tuki Tuki needed."

"It was risky," Bastille said, folding her arms.

"Yeah, but I don't think it was as dangerous as you say. Aydee's got one of the most powerful Prime Talents around, but I doubt she'd have been able to make *millions* of bears. Likely, she couldn't have destroyed the city—at best she'd have just crushed those of us here in this field."

"Very comforting," Bastille said dryly.

"Well, you know what my pop says. Danger, risks, and lots of fun. The Smedry way!"

Kaz, as I've mentioned, is a scholar of magical forces. He knew more about Talents than anyone else alive. In fact, that's probably what he'd been doing here when he'd visited Tuki Tuki originally—studying at the university.

"My Lord," Mink—the soda-can counselor—said, approaching. "This boon of bears is quite timely, but how are we going to use it to destroy those robots? They're protected by the Librarian army!"

"And don't forget the tunnels," Dink said.

"And always wash behind your ears," Wink added.

"I need three things from you," I said, thinking quickly. "Some backpacks that will hold several of those bears, six of your fastest warriors, and some really long stilts."

The counselors looked at each other.

"Go!" I said, waving. "That dome is about to fall!"

The three scattered, scrambling to do as I asked.

Bastille suddenly turned eastward, toward the ocean. Toward Nalhalla. Her eyes opened. "Alcatraz, I think the knights are actually coming."

"What? You can see them?" I looked eagerly.

"I can't see them," Bastille said. "I can *feel* them." She tapped the back of her neck, where the Fleshstone was set into her skin, hidden by her silvery hair. It connected her to the Crystin Mindstone, which then connected her to all of the other Knights of Crystallia.

I didn't see why they were so keen on the thing. I mean, it was because of that very connection that the Knights had all fallen to Archedis's tricks in Nalhalla. He'd done something to the Mindstone, and it—connected to all of the Crystin— had knocked them out. Seemed like a liability to me.

Of course, that connection was *also* able to turn thirteen-year-old girls into superknight kung-fu killing machines. So it wasn't all bad.

"You can sense the other knights?" I said, frowning.

"Only in the most general of terms," she said. "We . . . well, we don't talk about it. If a lot of them feel the same thing at once, I will notice it. And if a lot of them start moving at once, I can feel it. A large number of knights just left Nalhalla."

"They *just* left Nalhalla," I said, groaning inside. "The trip here will take hours and hours."

"We have to hold out," Bastille said, fervently. "Alcatraz, your plan is working! For once."

"Assuming we can survive for a few more hours," Kaz said. "You have a plan about that, kid?"

"Well," I said. "Kind of. Bastille, how good are you with stilts?"

"Um . . . okay, I guess." She hesitated. "I should be worried, shouldn't I?"

"Probably."

She sighed. "Ah well. It can't possibly be worse than death by teddy-bear avalanche." She hesitated again. "Can it?"

I just smiled.

Chapter

° Four Teens and a Pickle °

In March 1225, two years before his death, Genghis Khan sat down to breakfast to dine on a bowl of warm hearts cut from the chests of his enemies. At that time, he was ruler of the largest empire in the history of the world. He reached up, scratched his nose, and said something extremely profound.

"Zaremdaa, en ajil shall mea baina."

He knew what he was talking about. As do I. Trust me, I've been a king before. (No, really, I have. Sometime, check out volume four of my autobiography.)

I was only king of one city, really, and only for a short time. But it was ridiculously, insanely, bombastically tough to do the job right. Tougher than trying to get hit in the head with a baseball shot out of a cannon. Tougher than trying to climb a hundred-foot cliff using a rope made of used dental floss.

Tougher, even, than trying to figure out where my stoopid metaphors come from.

I've never understood one thing: Why do all of these megalomaniac dictators, secret societies, mad scientists, and totalitarian aliens *want* to rule the world? I mean really? Don't they know what a pain in the neck it is to be in charge? People are always making unreasonable demands of kings. "Please save us from the invading Vandal hordes! Please make sure we have proper sanitation to prevent the spread of disease! Please stop beheading your wives so often; it's ruining the rugs!"

Being a king is like getting your driver's license. It sounds really cool, but when you finally get your license, you realize that all it *really* means is that your parents can now make you drive your brothers and sisters to soccer practice.

Like Genghis Khan said. "Zaremdaa, en ajil shall mea baina." Or, translated, "Sometimes, this job sucks." But really, hasn't *everyone* said that at some point?

"Zaremdaa, en ajil shall mea baina!" Bastille said from way up high.

"What was that?" I called up. "I don't speak Mongolian."

"I said, sometimes my job really sucks!"

"You're doing great!"

"That doesn't mean that this doesn't *suck*!" Bastille called.

You see, at this point Bastille was balanced atop a set of stilts, which were in turn taped to another set of stilts, which

were in turn taped to *another* set of stilts. Those were on top of a chair, which was on top of a table. And all of that was balanced on top of the Mokian university's science building. (It was a large, island-bungalow-style structure. You know, the kind of place you'd expect to find Jimmy Buffett singing, Warren Buffett vacationing, or a pulled-pork buffet being served.)

"Do you see anything?" I called up to her.

"My entire life flashing before my eyes?"

"Besides that."

"It's really easy to see who's balding from up here."

"Bastille!" I said, annoyed.

"Sorry," she called down. "I'm just trying to distract myself from my impending death."

"You weren't so nervous when I suggested this!"

"I was on the *ground* then!"

I raised an eyebrow. I hadn't realized that Bastille was scared of heights. She hadn't acted like this before. Of course, other times she'd been up high, she'd been in a flying vehicle. Not strapped to three sets of stilts and balancing on a roof.

For all her complaining, she was doing a remarkable job, and *she* had been the one to suggest taping the stilts together to get her up higher. Besides, she was wearing her Glassweave jacket, which would save her if she did fall. Her Crystin abilities allowed her to keep her balance, despite the height and the instability of her position. It was rather remarkable.

Of course, that didn't stop me from wanting to tease her. "You aren't feeling dizzy, are you?"

"You aren't helping."

"Man, I think the breeze is picking up . . ."

"Shut up!"

"Is that an earthquake?"

"I'm going to kill you slowly when I get down from here. I'll do it with a hairpin. I'll go for your heart, by way of your foot."

I smiled. I shouldn't have taunted her. The situation was dire, and there was little cause for laughter in Tuki Tuki. The dome was cracking even further, and my counselors—the two somewhat useful ones, at least—said they thought it would last only another fifteen minutes or so.

But seeing Bastille in a situation like this—where she was uncomfortable and nervous—was very rare. I just . . . well, I had to do it. And that, by the way, is the definition of stoop-iderlifluous: being so stoopid as to taunt Bastille while she's out of arm's reach, assuming she won't get revenge very soon afterward.

As I smirked, Kaz rounded the building and trotted up to me, wearing his dark Warrior's Lenses. He'd gotten two small pistols somewhere and wore them strapped to his chest. They looked like flint and powder models, perhaps taken from the Mokian stores.

"Everything's ready," he said. "Mokians all over the city are climbing atop buildings, looking for the first sign of Librarian holes opening." He glanced up at Bastille. "I see you found a way to get even higher," he called at her. "Reason number fifty-six and a half: Short people know when to stay on the ground. We're closer to it; we appreciate it more. What is it with you tall people and extreme heights?"

"Kaz, I'm a thirteen-year-old girl," Bastille called down. "I'm only, like, a couple of inches taller than you are."

"It's the principle of the thing," he called back. Then he looked to me. "So, are you going to explain this plan of yours, kid?"

"Well, we've got two problems. The rocks hitting the shield and the tunnels digging up. We can't stop the rocks because there's an army between us and the robots. But the Librarians are conveniently digging tunnels from their rear lines up into our city. So one of the problems presents a solution to the other."

"Ah," Kaz said thoughtfully. "So those folks . . ." He nodded to the six Mokian runners Aluki had gotten for me. They stood in a line, ready to dash away, bearing backpacks filled with stuffed bears.

I nodded. "Usually after the Librarians are fought off from the hole they dig, the Mokians collapse the tunnel. But this time, as soon as the hole is spotted we'll move everyone out of the area. The emptiness will make the Librarians think that they haven't been noticed, and they'll rush out to cause mayhem. These six soldiers will then sneak down the tunnel and run out behind Librarian lines, then take down the robots. A single one of these bears to the leg should make the robot collapse."

"Wow," Kaz said. "That's actually a good plan."

"You sound surprised."

Kaz shrugged. "You're a Smedry, kid. Half our ideas are insane. The other half are insane but brilliant at the same time. Deciding which is which can be trouble sometimes."

"I'll tell you how to decide," Bastille called down. "Look and see which one involves *me* having to climb up a hundred feet in the air and balance on stilts. Shattering Smedrys!"

"How can she even *hear* us from up there?" Kaz muttered.

"I have very good ears!" Bastille called.

"Here," I said, picking up a backpack. "I made one of these for each of us too. There are two of each kind of bear in there. I figured we should all have some, just in case."

Kaz nodded, throwing on his backpack. I shrugged mine on as well.

"You realize," Kaz said softly, "that the soldiers you send out to stop those robots won't be returning."

"What? They could run back in the tunnel, and . . ."

And I trailed off, realizing how stoopid it sounded. The Librarians might get surprised by my tricky plan—*might*—but they'd never let the Mokian soldiers escape into the tunnel after destroying the robots. Even if all of this worked out exactly as I wanted, those six men and women weren't returning. At best, they'd get captured. Maybe knocked out by Librarian coma-bullets.

I hadn't considered this. Perhaps because I didn't want to. Go back and read the beginning of this chapter. Maybe now you'll start to understand what I was saying.

I glanced at the six soldiers. Their faces were grim but determined. They carried their packs over their shoulders, and each held a spear. They were younger soldiers, four men and two women, who Aluki had said were their fastest runners. I could see from their eyes that they understood. As

I regarded them, they nodded to me one at a time. They were ready to sacrifice themselves for Mokia.

They had seen what my request would demand of them, even if I hadn't. Suddenly, I felt very stoopiderliflifluous.

"I should cancel the plan," I said suddenly. "We can think of something else."

"Something that doesn't risk the lives of your soldiers?" Kaz said. "Kid, we're at *war*."

"I just . . ." I didn't want to be the one responsible for them going into danger. But there was nothing to be done about it. I sighed, sitting down.

Kaz joined me. "So now . . ." he said.

"Now we wait, I guess." I glanced upward nervously. The rocks continued to fall; the glass's cracks glowed faintly, making the dark night sky look like it was aglow with lightning. Fifteen minutes. If the Librarians didn't burrow in during the next fifteen minutes, the dome would shatter and the Librarian armies would rush in. Most of the Mokians—the ones I didn't have watching for tunnels—were already gathered on the wall, anticipating the attack.

I blinked, realizing for the first time how tired I was. It was well after eleven at this point, and the excitement of everything had kept me going. Now I just had to wait. In many ways, that seemed like the worst thing imaginable. Waiting, thinking, worrying.

Isn't it odd, how waiting can be both boring and nerve-racking at the same time? Must have something to do with quantum physics.

A question occurred to me, something I'd been wondering for a while. Kaz seemed the perfect person to ask. I shook off some of my tiredness. "Kaz," I said, "has any of the research you've done indicated that the Talents might be . . . alive?"

"What?" Kaz said, surprised.

I wasn't sure how to explain. Back in Nalhalla—when we'd been in the Royal Archives (not a library)—my Talent had done some odd things. At one point, it had seemed to *reach* out of me. Like it was alive. It had stopped my cousin Folsom from accidentally using his own Talent against me.

"I'm not sure what I mean," I said lamely.

"We've done a *lot* of research on Talents," Kaz said, drawing his little circle diagram in the dirt, the one that divided up different Talents into types and power ranges. "But we don't really *know* much."

"The Smedry line is the royal line of Incarna," I said. "An ancient race of people who mysteriously vanished."

"They didn't vanish," Kaz said. "They destroyed themselves somehow, until only our line remained. We lost the ability to read their language."

"The Forgotten Language," I said. "We didn't forget it.

Alcatraz the First *broke* it. The entire language. So that people couldn't read it. Why?"

"I don't know," Kaz said. "The Incarna were the first to get Talents."

"They brought them down into themselves, somehow," I said, thinking back to the words of Alcatraz the First, which I'd discovered in his tomb in the Library of Alexandria. "It was like . . . Kaz, I think what they were trying to do was create people who could *mimic* the power of Oculatory Lenses. Only without having to use the Lenses."

Kaz frowned. "What makes you say that?"

"My tongue moving while breath moves out of my lungs and through my throat, vibrating my vocal cords and—"

"I *meant*," Kaz said. "Why do you think that the Talents are like Lenses?"

"Oh. Right. Well, a lot of the Talents do similar things to Lenses. Like Australia's Talent and Disguiser's Lenses. I did some reading on it while I was in Mokia. There are a lot of similarities. Shatterer's Lenses can break other glass if you look at it; that's kind of like my Talent. And then there are Traveler's Lenses, which can push a person from one point to another and ignore obstructions in between. That's kind of like what you do. I wonder if there are Lenses that work like Grandpa's power, slowing things or making them late."

"There are," Kaz said thoughtfully. "Educator's Lenses. When you put them on, it slows time."

"That's an odd name."

"Not really. Have you ever known anything that can slow down time like a boring class at school?"

"Good point," I said.

All in all, there were thousands of different kinds of glass that had been identified. A lot of them—like the Traveler's Lenses—were impractical to use. They were either too dangerous, took too much energy to work, or were so rare that complete Lenses of them were nearly impossible to forge.

"Some glass is called technology," I said, "but that's just because it can be powered by brightsand. But all glass can be powered by Oculators. I've done it before."

"I know," Kaz said. "The boots. You said you were able to give them an extra jolt of power."

"I did it again," I said. "With Transporter's Glass in Nalhalla."

"Curious," Kaz said. "But Al, nobody else can do that. What makes you think this involves the Incarna?"

"Well, neurons in my brain transmit an electrochemical signal to one another and—"

"I *mean*," Kaz interrupted. "Why do you think this has something to do with the Incarna."

"Because," I said. "I just have a feeling about it. Partially

Alcatraz the First's writings, partially instinct. The Incarna knew about all these kinds of glass, but they wanted more. They wanted to have these powers innate inside of people. And so somehow, they made it happen—they *gave* us Talents. They turned us into Lenses, kind of."

I frowned. "Maybe it's not the fact that I'm an Oculator that lets me power glass. Maybe it's the fact that I'm an Oculator *and* a Smedry. That's much rarer, isn't it?"

"I only know of four who are both," Kaz said. "You, Pop, your father, and Australia."

"Has any research been done into people like us powering glass?"

"Not that I know of," he confessed.

"I'm right, Kaz," I said. "I can *feel* it. The Incarna did something to themselves, something that ended with the creation of the Smedry Talents."

Kaz nodded slowly.

"Aren't you going to ask what makes me feel this way?"

"Wasn't planning on it."

"'Cuz I've got this really great comment prepared on the unconscious mind interacting with the conscious mind and releasing chemical indicators in the form of hormones that influence an emotional response."

"Glad I didn't ask, then," Kaz noted.

"Ah well."

Now, it may seem odd to you that I—a boy of merely thirteen years—figured out all that stuff about the Incarna, when scholars had been trying for centuries to discover it. I had some advantages, though. First, I had the unusual position of being a Smedry, an Oculator, and a holder of the Breaking Talent. From what I can determine, there hadn't been someone who had possessed all three for thousands of years. I might have been the only one other than Alcatraz the First.

Because of that unusual combination, I'd done some strange things. (You've seen me do some of them in these books.) I'd seen things others hadn't, and that had led me to conclusions they couldn't have made. Beyond that, I'd *read* what many of the other scholars—like Kaz—had written. That's part of what I'd spent my time doing in Nalhalla while I waited for the fourth book to start.

There's a saying in the Hushlands. "If I have seen further it is only by standing on the shoulders of giants." Newton said it first. I'm not sure how he got hit on the head with an apple while standing up so high in the air, but the quote is quite good.

I had all of their research. I had my own knowledge. Adding it all up, I happened to figure out the right answer.

Kaz nodded to himself, slowly. "I think you might be on to something, kid. Some scholars have noticed the connection between types of Smedry Talents and types of glass. They've even tried to put the glasses onto the Incarnate Wheel. But your explanation goes a step further."

He tapped the diagram he'd drawn on the floor. "I like it. Things tend to make sense once you figure out all of the pieces. We call Smedry Talents 'magic.' But I've never liked that word. The Talents work according to their own rules. Take Aydee's power, for instance."

"It seems pretty magical," I admitted. "Creating five thousand bears out of thin air?"

"She didn't create them out of nothing," Kaz said. "She's got a spatial Talent, one that changes how things are in space with relation to other things. Like my Talent. I get lost. This moves me from one place to another. Your father loses things, not himself. He can tuck something into his pocket, and it will be gone the next moment. But when he really needs it, he'll 'find' it in the pocket of a completely different outfit.

"Aydee's Talent is very similar to these. Those bears, they didn't come from nowhere. She moved them from someplace. Out of a storehouse or factory; perhaps she drained the armory in Nalhalla. That's how it always works. She's not magically making them appear; she's moving them here, and she's putting something back in their place—usually just empty air."

"Like Transporter's Glass," I said.

"Yes, actually," Kaz said. "Now that you mention it, that *is* very similar." He tapped the ground again. "So, if I get you right, you're saying that the Incarna turned people into Lenses. But something went wrong."

"Right," I said. "That's why the Talents are hard to control, why they do such odd things some of the time."

"And that's what your father is chasing, I warrant," Kaz said. "Didn't he say he wanted to give every person Smedry Talents?"

"Yeah," I said. "He announced it in a big press conference, to all of Nalhalla."

"He wants the secret," Kaz said.

"And my mother does too," I guessed. "It's hidden in the Forgotten Language. The trick, the method the Incarna used to turn *people* into *Lenses*. Kind of."

"And this whole issue with the Translator's Glass was based on that," Kaz said, growing excited. "Your mother and he were searching for this same secret, and they knew they needed to be able to read the Forgotten Language to find it. So they searched out the Sands of Rashid . . ."

"And broke up because of differences in how they planned to use the abilities once they found them," I said, glancing toward where my mother was locked up. "I have to talk to her, interrogate her. Maybe I can figure out if this is all correct."

Above us, Bastille began to swear.

I looked up; Bastille was pointing urgently. "Alcatraz! The earth is moving in a yard three streets over! I think Librarians are tunneling in over there!"

Kaz leaped to his feet, and the six Mokian runners came alert. My mother's interrogation would have to wait.

"Let's go!" I said, dashing in the direction Bastille had pointed.

Chapter

8675309

By now, you're probably confused at what chapter this is. Some people I let read the book early were a little confused by the chapter numbers. (Wimps.)

I did this intentionally. See, I knew it would drive Librarians crazy. Despite our many efforts to hide these books as innocent "fantasy" novels in the bookstores and libraries, the Librarians have proven too clever (or at least too meticulous) for us. They are reading my biographies, and perhaps learning too much about me. So it was time to employ some careful misdirection.

I considered writing the whole book in L33t, but felt that would give me too much m4d ski11z. So it came to the chapter numbers. As you have probably noticed, Librarians don't conform to most people's stereotypes. Most of them don't even *have* stereos. Beyond that, they're not sweet, book-loving scholars; they're maniacal cultists bent on ruling the world. They don't like to shush people. (Unless it means quieting them permanently by sinking them in the bay with their feet tied to an iron shelving cart.) In fact, most Librarians I've seen are quite fond of loud explosions, particularly the types that involve a Smedry at the center.

People don't become Librarians because they want to force people to be quiet, or because they love books, or because they want to help people. No, people become Librarians for only one reason: They like to put things in order. Librarians are *always* organizing stuff. They can't help it. You'll see them for hours and hours sitting on little stools in libraries, going over each and every book on their shelf, trying to decide if it should be moved over one or two slots. It drives them crazy when we normal people wander into their libraries and mess stuff up.

And so, I present to you the perfect Librarian trap. They'll come along, pick up this book and start to read it, thinking they're so smart for discovering my biography. The chapter numbers will be completely messed up. That, of course, will make their brains explode. So if you have to wipe some gray stuff off the book, you know who read it before you.

Sorry about that.

Once again I charged through the city, small retinue in

tow. Being king sure seemed to involve running around in the dark a lot.

"Kid," Kaz said, jogging beside me, "I should be on the strike team to attack the robots."

"What?" I exclaimed. "No, Kaz. I need you here."

"No you don't. You're doing just fine on your own."

"But—"

"Kid, with these Warrior's Lenses on, I can run faster than any of those Mokian soldiers."

That was true; Warrior's Lenses augmented a person's physical abilities. Kaz had no trouble keeping up with the rest of us, despite his shorter legs.

Warrior's Lenses were one of the few types that could be used by anyone, not just Oculators. It's proof that the world is unfair that I, to this day, have never had a chance to use Warrior's Lenses. (Well, except that once, but we won't talk about that.) They're supposedly beneath Oculators, or something like that.

"So give the Lenses to someone else," I said stubbornly.

"Wouldn't work," he replied. "They take a lot of training to learn to use. I'll bet there aren't more than a few dozen Mokian soldiers who can use them. Otherwise the entire army would be wearing them."

Oh. Well, that made sense. Unfortunately.

"Besides, kid," Kaz said, "I can use my Talent to escape

from behind the Librarian lines. I might even be able to pull a few of the other runners with me. If you send me, it'll save lives."

Now *that* was a good argument. If Kaz could get some of the runners out, then that would alleviate my conscience big time.

"Are you sure you can get out?" I said softly as we ran. "Your Talent has been unpredictable lately . . ."

"Oh, I'll be able to get out," Kaz said. "I just can't promise when I'll get back. The Talents . . . seems like they've *all* been acting up lately. Aydee's goes off at the mere mention of a number, and from what Bastille tells me, your father is losing things more and more often. Something's up."

I nodded, thinking again of how my Talent had seemed to *snap* out of my body at Folsom.

"All right, you're on the team," I said. Something occurred to me at that moment. "But after you get lost, don't try to come back here. Go to Grandpa Smedry instead. I want you to deliver a message for me."

"Sure thing," Kaz said.

"Tell him that we really, *really* need him here by midnight. If he doesn't arrive by then, we're doomed."

"Midnight?" Kaz said. "That's only a few minutes away."

"Just do it."

Kaz shrugged. "Okay."

We reached an intersection between two rows of pastoral homes and hesitated. Which way to go? Only Bastille knew. A second later she raced by, leading the way to the right. We followed her; it certainly hadn't taken her long to get down from the stilts and catch up.

At the end of a row of houses, she slowed and raised a hand. We bunched up behind her, and Kaz quietly informed the youngest—and most nervous-looking—of the Mokian runners that he'd been booted from the strike team. The youth looked very relieved.

"There," Bastille hissed, pointing at a section of ground several houses down. We peeked around the corner, watching as some shovels broke up out of the earth. The grass lowered, and moments later a few Librarian heads peeked out.

"Go get Aluki and his soldiers," I whispered to the young runner that Kaz had relieved. "Warn him about these infiltrators; he'll need to take care of them once the strike team has sneaked into the tunnel."

The runner nodded, dashing off. I peeked back around the corner. The Librarians were timidly glancing about, as if surprised to find no resistance. Several of them climbed out of the hole, slinking to the wall of the nearest hut. They waved for the others, and soon the entire group had exited the hole. They ran off down a side street, carrying their rifles

and looking for mayhem. In a lot of ways, these Librarian infiltration groups were suicide missions, just like my strike team. The difference being that the Librarians anticipated taking the city very soon, and finding the Mokian coma antidote.

"All right," I said, waving. "Go!"

Kaz and the five runners charged around the side of the building, running toward the hole. I waited anxiously. Were the Librarians far enough away? Would they notice what we were doing?

Bastille waited beside me, though I could tell she itched to leap forward and join the strike team. Fortunately, her primary duty was to protect me, so she restrained herself.

The strike team reached the hole and Kaz waved the runners to jump in. Suddenly, something flashed in the hole.

"Rifle fire!" Bastille said.

She was moving a moment later, bolting toward the hole. One of our runners collapsed backward, twitching. The others leaped for the ground, taking cover, and two Librarians peeked out of the hole, holding rifles.

Kaz whipped out a pistol and shot one in the face—it let out a blast of light, knocking the Librarian unconscious. Bastille—running inhumanly fast—arrived and kicked the other Librarian in the face.

I blinked. Things happened so *quickly* in battle. By the

time I thought to jog out, the two Librarian guards had been disabled. Unfortunately, one of our runners was down.

"Woodpeckers!" Kaz cursed. "We should have known they'd be smart enough to leave a rear guard." He checked on the runner who'd been shot. He was unconscious. We'd need the antidote to awaken him.

"There will probably be guards at the end of the tunnel as well," one of the Mokians said. "And while we're fast, we're not the best soldiers in the army."

Kaz nodded. "If you fight and make a disturbance, the Librarians will cut off our exit out of the tunnel. Sparrows!"

"Kaz, where did you pick up all that fowl language?" Bastille asked.

"Sorry. Spent two weeks trapped in an ornithologist's convention during my last time lost."

And that is a story all unto itself.

"Well," I said, "we'll just have to hope that . . ." I trailed off as I noticed Bastille and Kaz sharing a look. Then, shockingly, Bastille pulled the bear-containing backpack off the unconscious runner. She slung it over her shoulder, then looked at me.

"Stay here," she said.

"Bastille, no! You can't go."

"I have the best chance at knocking out guards at the exit

of the tunnel quietly. My speed and strength will let me get to those robots faster than the others. I need to go."

"But you're supposed to protect me!"

She pointed upward, at the glass dome. "It's only minutes away from breaking. This *is* the best way to protect you."

She secured her Warrior's Lenses. "Take care of yourself," she said. "You'd better not die. I'm getting a little fond of you. Besides, if I fall, you'll need to get me the antidote."

With that, she jumped down into the hole. I scrambled up to the edge, looking down. The drop wasn't a deep one; the tunnel quickly turned to the side as it pointed out toward the Librarian army. The runners jumped in after her. Kaz patted my arm. "I'll try to get her out, kid," he said.

He followed the others down into the hole, backpack carried over one arm, a pistol held warily in the other hand. He disappeared into the darkness.

I stared after them for several heartbeats, trying to sort through my emotions. I had sent a team out on a suicide mission. Me. They were following my orders. And *Kaz* and *Bastille* were with them.

Was this what it was to be a king? This terrible guilt?

It felt like someone had slathered all of my internal organs with honey, then let a jar full of ants loose inside there.

It felt like someone had shoved firecrackers up my nose, then set them off with a flame thrower.

It felt like being forced to eat a hundred rotting fish sticks.

In other words, it didn't feel so good.

I turned and took off at a dash, as quickly as I could. I passed Aluki and his soldiers fighting a pitched battle with the Librarians who'd left the tunnel. Running with all I had, I eventually reached the steps to the top of the wooden wall. I leaped up them. Then, out of breath, puffing, I slammed up against the front of the wall, looking out.

I arrived just in time to see the strike team erupt out of the other side of the tunnel. Bastille had dealt with the Librarian guards in her characteristically efficient way, and the soldiers outside of the tunnel didn't hear anything. They stood by stoopidly as the team of six runners poured from the tunnel and scattered in different directions.

A boulder crashed against the dome. Another chunk of glass broke free and fell inward, crushing a nearby home.

Come on, I thought anxiously, watching the runners. Mokians gathered around me, cheering them on. I noticed absently that my three "advisers" were among the crowd.

The six runners seemed so insignificant compared with the Librarian army. I found myself holding my breath, wishing there was something—anything—I could do to help. But I was inside the dome, and they far outside of it, an army between us. I could barely see them . . .

See them.

You're an Oculator, stoopid! Bastille's voice seemed to scream into my mind. I cursed to myself, fumbling in the pocket of my jacket, pulling out a set of glasses with a purple and green tint.

My Bestower's Lenses. Hurriedly, I pulled off my Oculator's Lenses and shoved on the Bestower's Lenses instead. Bastille had said, "They let you give something of yourself to someone else."

Let's see what these babies can do, I thought with determination.

The strike team spread out, one member heading for each of the robots. Those robots were distant enough from one another that each runner had to pick one robot and make for it. Fortunately, that put them running away from the bulk of the army, so they had to contend with only the smaller number of Librarians who were walking about near the back lines.

That was still a lot of Librarians. Hundreds. Bastille shoved one aside as he tried to attack her, then swung her sword into the stomach of a second.

The sword, it should be noted, did not have a magical "stunning" setting like the spears did. Ew.

Bastille continued on, but one of the Mokian runners was quickly getting surrounded. He looked kind of like a running back from American football, galloping down the field with a group of Librarian thugs trying to tackle him, a teddy bear held protectively in the crook of his arm.

I focused on him, channeling strength through my Bestower's Lenses. I suddenly felt weak, and my legs started quivering. But I remained focused, and the Mokian took off in a burst of speed, getting ahead of the Librarians, who stumbled and tripped into a mess of arms and legs.

I quickly sought out the other runners. Kaz dodged to the side of a group of Librarians, neatly using his pistol to pick off the one running at him from the front. But one of the other Mokians had gotten into a predicament. A crowd of Librarians was in front of her, shoulder to shoulder. They seemed intent on capturing her rather than shooting her down, which was good.

She looked desperate, and she crouched down to try a final leap before crashing into the Librarians. I focused on her, then jumped into the air, channeling the leap through my Bestower's Lenses into her. She jumped, and my jump added to hers. She bounded into the air, narrowly leaping over the shocked Librarians' heads, while I jumped only an inch or so.

I landed, smiling. Another of the runners was slamming into a group of Librarians that were blocking him; with my help he pushed straight through, knocking them to the ground.

I've been told that I shouldn't have been able to accomplish what I did with those Lenses. Theoretically, I would have added only a little bit of strength—as much as a thirteen-year-old boy could manage—to the Mokians. My strength added to that of the willowy runner shouldn't have let him knock down three toughened Librarian thugs.

But it did. This time, for once in my narrative, I'm not lying. However, that bit about the giant, enchanted ninja wombat was totally made up.

My heart thumped; I felt like I was down there, running for my life. I jumped back and forth between the six runners, eyes flicking here, then there, granting them whatever I could. At one point, one of the runners was confronted by a group of Librarians leveling guns.

You can do it! I thought at the runner, sending all of the courage I could muster.

The runner suddenly looked ten times more confident. He stared down the guns and managed to dodge between them as I granted him extra dexterity, leeching it from myself. He got to the Librarian gunners and leaped over their heads as I enhanced his ability to jump.

The rest of the Librarian armies had noticed what was happening. Hundreds of soldiers charged from the front lines, yelling. But most were too far away.

Bastille reached her robot. I held my breath as she tossed her grenade bear.

It hit.

I couldn't hear the explosion, but it vaporized the entire

section of metal beneath the robot's knee. The robot teetered, holding a rock that it had been about to throw. Then it toppled backward.

Even inside Tuki Tuki, we felt the vibrations of it hitting the ground. A monstrous, powerful *thump*. To me, it felt like the fall of Goliath. (If Goliath had been felled by a purple teddy bear.)

The Mokians on the wall around me let out a loud cheer of victory. On the far side of the Librarian field, Kaz reached his robot. Though he and Bastille had taken the two robots farthest away on either side, their Warrior's Lenses had let them arrive first.

Kaz tossed his bear into the robot's calf, then dashed away as the monstrous creation fell to the ground, crushing trees beneath it with an awful sound. Kaz jumped into the air in pleasure, probably letting out a whoop of joy at felling the biggest big person of them all. I could almost hear him scream out: "Reason number three thousand forty-seven! Little people don't feel the need to build their robots as tall as buildings! Ha!"

He took off at a gallop toward the other runners. I smiled broadly, checking on them.

And that was when the first Mokian I had helped got shot in the back.

Chapter

16

Stoopid, elegant, skinny, odd, extravagant.

These words all share something, something you're not expecting. If you can figure it out, I'll give you a cookie. (The answer is at the beginning of the next chapter.)

I'll give you a hint: It has to do with the meaning of the word "awful."

"No!" I said, watching as the Mokian tumbled to the ground, dropping his bear and rolling to a stop. The Librarians rushed up behind him, surrounding him and prodding him with their rifles. He was out cold.

Just like that, the plan fell apart. Another robot dropped as one of the three remaining runners hit their target. Another soon followed, leaving only two robots standing.

But that was enough. Another rock fell, and a chunk of glass nearby cracked free.

I looked up. There were so many cracks in the dome that I could barely see the sky.

"I'd guess one more rock will drop it," Mink the adviser said from beside me. "Two at the most."

"We can't let that happen!" I said. The two remaining robots were lifting arms to throw. Another of the runners fell—one that had already destroyed her robot—blasted in the side by Librarians.

Guns were firing all over now, flashing in the night like the lights of some insane disco. I guess the Librarians finally realized what we were doing—at first they likely thought we were just trying to get messengers out.

A Mokian still darted toward one of the remaining robots. Gun blasts fell around him. "Run!" I said, focusing on him. Giving him strength, speed, jumping ability, everything I could leech out of myself. He dodged about on fleet feet, inhumanly fast. But a contingent of Librarian riflemen set up just beside him.

"NO!" I screamed louder, letting out a *jolt* of something through my Lenses. I could almost see it. A black arrow that streaked through the air, striking the Mokian.

The Librarians pulled triggers. And their guns exploded.

I froze, shocked, as the Mokian runner leaped in one final bound over a fallen log, then threw his bear. It smacked into the robot's leg, exploding. The robot tried to throw its boulder, but didn't have the leverage, and the stone fell to the ground out of its grasp. The robot followed, crashing to the earth.

The Mokian skidded to a stop, and a Librarian shot him a moment later, knocking him out.

That was my Talent, I realized. *For a brief moment, I used the Lenses to grant that runner my Talent. It broke the guns when they tried to fire on him.*

The last remaining robot tossed his boulder. We all held our breaths as it flew, then smashed into the dome, crashing through it completely and falling into the city. Shards of glass rained down on us. It left a gaping hole in the roof.

Outside, the Librarians cheered. Behind them I noticed three scrambling forms congregating. Kaz had met up with the two remaining Mokian runners. Kaz hesitated just briefly, but obviously realized that he couldn't wait any longer. A Librarian's rifle shot hit the ground next to them, spraying up dirt and smoke, giving Kaz the moment of disorientation he needed to engage his Talent. As the smoke passed, the three of them were gone, carried to safety.

The last robot leaned down to get another boulder. The hole in the ceiling was bad enough; this final boulder would shatter the dome entirely. Around me, the Mokians hushed as the final robot raised the enormous rock. The Librarians below moved into their attack lines, preparing to assault Tuki Tuki.

My eyes caught something. Motion. There, rushing across the ground behind the Librarian lines, was a small determined figure with silver hair. Bastille.

There was still hope.

The Mokians noticed her, pointing. Bastille—belligerent Bastille—had ignored safety, choosing to run for that last robot instead of trying to get to Kaz. She charged with sword sheathed at her waist, Warrior's Lenses on, dashing with Crystin speed through, around, and sometimes *over* confused Librarian soldiers.

"She's not going to make it," Aluki said softly. The robot raised its boulder. "It's too late . . ."

He was right. That robot would throw before Bastille arrived. "She needs more time. I need to get down there." My heart beating quickly, I moved by instinct, shoving my way through the Mokians and rushing down the steps to the ground. I ran up to the gate out of the city.

"Open the gate!" I cried.

The guards looked at me, dumbfounded. I didn't have time to argue, so I brushed past them and slammed my hands against the gate, sending my Talent into it. The bar holding the gate closed shattered into about a billion splinters, the force of the explosion sending the gates swinging open.

I rushed out the door and realized something important. Something life changing. Something amazing.

I needed a battle cry.

"Rutabaga!" I screamed.

It's the first thing that came to mind, I'm afraid. Anyway, I dashed out across the grassy ground, running to the edge of the glass dome. Outside, the robot snapped its massive arms forward, launching the boulder.

I came right up to the glass of the protective shield. Taking a deep breath, I placed my hands against it and sent a surge of power into it.

The dome in front of me let out a wave of light, a ripple of energy. I closed my eyes, holding my hands to the smooth surface, power surging through me like luminescent blood pumping into the glass.

For a moment I felt like I *was* the glass dome protecting the city. I strengthened the dome, giving it an extra boost, like I'd done with the Transporter's Glass months before.

The rock hit.

And it bounced off, the dome unharmed. I opened my eyes to find the entire thing glowing with a brilliant, beautiful light.

Power was flowing through me at an alarming rate. It seemed to be towing bits of me along with it, my strength, even my soul. I could feel the Talent coiled inside, wanting to snap forth and *destroy* the very thing I was trying to protect. I had to forcibly hold it back.

At no point in my life up to this moment had my dual nature—Oculator and Smedry—been so pointedly manifest to me. In one hand I held the power to save Mokia, and in the other hand the power to destroy it.

I forced myself to release the glass, stumbling backward, exhausted and drained. I felt like I'd just run a marathon

while carrying Atlas on my shoulders. And boy, that guy's gained *weight* over the years. (Due to all those new stars we've discovered in the sky, you see.)

I fell to the ground, exhausted, Mokians swarming around me. I waved them away, but let Aluki help me to my feet. The robot was getting another boulder. Where was Bastille?

She'd been caught by a large group of Librarians. She fought desperately, waving her sword around her, fending off the soldiers. She seemed to glance in our direction, then she turned, pulling a bear from her pack and whipping it into the air.

The maneuver exposed her back to the Librarians.

"Bastille . . ." I said, raising a hand. I tried to send her strength through the Bestower's Lenses, but I was too weak. A dozen different shots from Librarian guns hit her at once.

Bastille dropped.

The bear soared.

I held my breath as the robot raised its rock. I didn't have the strength to protect the city again.

And . . . . .

And . . . .

And . . .

And . .

And .

And..

And...

And....

And.....

The bear hit dead on. A large section of the robot's leg vaporized and it teetered, then toppled to the side, dropping its rock.

Around me, the Mokians let out relieved breaths. I wasn't paying attention. I was just looking at Bastille, lying unconscious on the ground. The Librarians were raising their guns in excitement, as if they'd just felled some fearsome beast. Which I guess they had.

The Librarians pulled Bastille's jacket off her and began shooting it over and over with their guns. That confused me until I realized they must have recognized it as Glassweave. These soldiers belonged to the Order of the Shattered Lens, and they hated glass of all types. They took off her Lenses and shot those a few times too.

Of course, their hatred of glass didn't explain why they felt the need to start kicking Bastille in the stomach as she lay there unconscious. I watched, teeth clenched tightly, seething with hatred and anger as they beat on Bastille for a few minutes. I almost ran right out there to go for her, but Aluki caught my arm. He knew that there was no good in it. I'd just get myself captured too.

The Librarians then picked her up and hauled her away as a prize of war. It was a special victory for them, catching a Knight of Crystallia. They took her to a tent at the rear of the battlefield, where they stored all of the important captives they'd put into comas. I felt a coward for having let her go out there without me, and for not going to get her when she fell.

"Your Majesty?" Aluki said to me. The Mokians around me had grown quiet. They seemed to be able to sense my mood. Perhaps it was because I was unconsciously causing the ground around me to crack and break.

I was alone. No Grandpa, no Bastille, no Kaz. Sure, I had Aluki and his soldiers, not to mention Aydee back in the city. But for the first time in a long while I felt alone, without guidance.

At this point you're probably expecting me to say something bitter. Something like, "I never should have become so dependent on others. That only set me up to fail."

Or maybe, "Losing Bastille was inevitable, after I was put in charge. I should never have taken the kingship."

Or maybe you want me to say, "Help, there is a snake eating my toes and I forgot to take the jelly out of the oven." (If so, I can't believe you wanted me to say that. You're a sick, sick person. What does that even mean? Weirdo.)

Anyway, I will say none of those things here. The fact

that you were expecting them means I've trained you well enough.

Now excuse me while I fetch my snake repellant.

"Are you all right, Your Majesty?" Aluki asked again, timid.

"We *will* win this battle," I said. I felt a strange sense of determination shoving away my feelings of shame and loss. "And we *will* get the antidote. We no longer have an option." I turned to regard the soldiers. "We will find a way to get Bastille out, and then wake her up. I am *not* going to fail her."

The soldiers nodded solemnly. Oddly, in that moment I finally *felt* like a Smedry, maybe even a king, for the first time.

"The city is protected for the time being," I said. "Though we still have to worry about the tunnels. I want people back to their posts watching the city for Librarian incursions. We're going to last. We're going to win. I vow it."

"Your Majesty," Aluki said, nodding upward. "They knocked a hole in the dome. They'll find a way to exploit that."

"I know," I said. "We'll deal with that when it happens. Have someone watch to see what the Librarians do next. Ask my advisers if they can think of any way to patch that hole."

"Yes, Your Majesty," Aluki said. "Er . . . what will you be doing?"

I took a deep breath. "It's time to confront my mother."

Chapter

° NCC-1701 °

In the year 1288, if you were to pass by an old acquaintance on the way to Ye Olde Chainmail Shoppe and call him "nice," you'd actually be calling him an idiot.

If it were the year 1322 instead—and you were on your way to the bookshop to pick up the new wacky comedy by a guy named Dante—when you called someone "nice" you would be saying that they were timid.

In 1380, if you called someone "nice," you'd be saying they were fussy.

In 1405, you'd be calling them dainty.

In 1500, you'd be calling them careful.

By the 1700s—when you were off to do some crowd surfing at the new Mozart concert—you'd be using the word "nice" to mean agreeable.

Sometimes it's difficult to understand how much change there is all around us. Even language changes, and the same word can mean different things depending on how, where, and when it was said. The word "awful" used to mean deserving of awe—full of awe. The same as "awesome." Once, the word "brave" meant cowardly. The word "girl" meant a child of either gender.

(So next time you're with a mixed group of friends, you should call them "girls" instead of "guys." Assuming you're not too brave, nice, nice, nice, or nice.)

People change too. In fact, they're always changing. We like to pretend that the people we know stay the same, but they change moment by moment as they come to new conclusions, experience new things, think new thoughts. Perhaps, as Heraclitus said, you can never step in the same river twice . . . but I think a more powerful metaphor would have been this: You can never meet the same person twice.

The Mokians hadn't put my mother in the university with the other prisoners. I'd told them to put her in a place that was very secure, but they didn't have a prison. (It may surprise you to learn this. Mokia is exactly the sort of place the Librarians don't want you to believe in. A paradise where people are learned, where arguments don't turn into fistfights—they turn into debates over warm tea and grapes.)

No, the Mokians didn't have a prison. But they *did* have a zoo.

It was actually more of a research farm, a place where exotic animals could be kept and studied in the name of science. My mother, Shasta Smedry, was confined in a large cage with thick bars that looked like it had once been used to house a tiger or other large cat. It had a little pool for water, a tree to climb in, and several large rock formations.

Unfortunately, the Mokians had removed the tiger before locking my mother in. That was probably for the tiger's safety.

I walked toward the cage, two Mokian guards at my side. Shasta sat inside on a small rock, legs crossed primly, wearing her Librarian business suit with the ankle-length gray skirt and high-necked white blouse. She had on horn-rimmed glasses. They weren't magical, according to my Oculator's Lenses. I checked just to be certain.

"Mother," I said flatly, stepping up to the cage.

"Son," she replied.

I should note that this felt very, *very* odd. I'd once confronted my mother in a situation almost exactly like this, during my very first Library infiltration. Except then my mother had been the one outside the bars, and I had been the one behind them.

I didn't feel any safer having it this way.

"I need to know the formula for the antidote," I told her.

"The one that will overcome the effects of the Librarian coma-guns."

"It's a pity, then," she said, "that I don't have it."

I narrowed my eyes. "I don't believe you."

"Hmm . . . If only there were a way for you to tell if I were speaking lies or not."

I blushed, then dug out my Truthfinder's Lens. I looked through it.

She spoke directly at me. "I don't know the antidote."

The words puffed from her mouth like white clouds. She was telling the truth. I felt a sinking feeling.

"I'm not from the Order of the Shattered Lens," my mother continued. "They wouldn't entrust one such as me with something that important—they wouldn't let *any* foot soldier know it. That secret will be very carefully guarded, as will the secret of the antidote to the Mokian stun-spears."

I looked at my guards. Aluki nodded. "Very few know our formula, Your Majesty. One was the queen, and the other is the—"

"Don't say it," I said, eyeing my mother.

She just rolled her eyes. "You think I care about this little dispute, Alcatraz? I haven't the faintest interest in the outcome of this siege."

It was the truth.

I gritted my teeth in annoyance. "Then why did you sneak in?"

She just smiled at me. An insufferable, knowing smile. She'd been the one to suggest I get out my Truthfinder's Lens. She wasn't going to be tricked into saying anything condemning. At least, not unless I shocked her or distracted her.

"I know what you and Father are doing," I said. "The Sands of Rashid, the book you both wanted from Nalhalla."

"You don't know anything."

"I know that you're seeking the secret of Smedry Talents," I said. "You married my father to get access to a Talent, to study them, and perhaps to get close to the whole family. It was always about the Talents. And now you're looking to discover the way that the Incarna people got *their* Talents in the first place."

She studied me. Something I'd said actually seemed to make her hesitate, to look at me in a new way. "You've changed, Alcatraz."

"Yeah, I put a new pair on this morning."

She rolled her eyes again, then stood up. "Put away that Lens, leave your guards behind, and let's have a chat."

"What? Why would I do that!"

"Because you should obey your mother."

"My mother is a ruthless, malevolent, egocentric Librarian bent on controlling the world!"

"We all have our faults," she said, strolling away from me, following the line of bars to the right. "Do as I request, or I'll remain silent. The choice is yours."

I ground my teeth, but there didn't seem to be any other choice. Reluctantly, I put the Truthfinder's Lens away and waved at the guards to remain behind as I hurried after Shasta. I wouldn't be able to tell if she was lying or not, at least not for certain. But I hoped I could still learn something from her. Why had she joined the group infiltrating Tuki Tuki? Perhaps she knew something, some way to save us.

As I moved to join her, an alarm rang through the city—one of the scouts we'd posted had seen a tunnel opening. Hopefully the soldiers would be able to deal with it. I walked up to where Shasta stood, far enough from Aluki and the other guard to be out of earshot. I suspected that she wanted me away from those two so she could manipulate me into letting her go free.

That wasn't going to happen. I hadn't forgotten how she'd given Himalaya up to be executed, nor how she'd sold me—her own son—to Blackburn, the one-eyed Dark Oculator. Or how she killed Asmodean. (Okay, so she didn't really do that last one, but I wouldn't put it past her.)

"What is it you think you know about the Smedry Talents?"

she said to me, arms folded. Her smirk was gone; she looked serious now, perhaps somewhat ominous. The effect was spoiled by the giant tiger chew toy in the grass beside her.

"Kaz and I talked it through," I said. "The Incarna wanted to turn *people* into *Lenses*."

She sniffed. "A crude way of putting it. They discovered the source of of magic in Lenses. Every person's soul has a *power* to it, an *energy*. Lenses don't have any inherent energy; what they do is focus the energy of the Oculator, distort it, change it into something useful. Like a prism refracting light."

She looked at me. "The eyes are the key," she said. "Poets have called them windows to the soul. Well, windows go both directions—someone can look into your eyes and see your soul, but when you look at someone, the energy of your soul shines forth. If there are Lenses in front of that energy, it distorts into something else. In some cases it changes what is going *in*to your eyes, letting you see things you couldn't normally. In other cases it changes what comes *out*, creating bursts of fire or wind."

"That's nonsense," I said. "I've had Lenses that worked even after I took them off."

"Your soul was still feeding them," she said. "For some kinds of glass, looking through them is important. For others, being near your soul alone is enough, and merely touching them can activate them."

"Why are you telling me this?"

"You will see," she said cryptically.

I didn't trust her. I don't think anyone with half a brain would trust Shasta Smedry.

"So what of the Incarna?" I asked.

"They wanted to harness this energy of the soul," she said. "Every person's soul vibrates with a distinctive tone, just like pure crystal will create a tone if rubbed the right way. The Incarna felt they could change the soul's vibration to manifest its energy. Men would not 'become Lenses' as you put it. Instead, they'd be able to use the power of their soul vibrations."

The power of their soul vibrations? That sounds like a '70s disco song, doesn't it? I really need to start a band or something to play all of these hits.

"All right," I said. "But something went wrong, didn't it? The Talents were flawed. Instead of getting the powers the Incarna anticipated, they ended up with a bunch of people who could barely control their abilities."

"Yes," she said, looking at me, thoughtful. "You've considered this a great deal."

I felt a surge of rebellious pride. My mother—known as Ms. Fletcher during my childhood—had very rarely given me anything resembling a compliment.

"You want the Talents for yourself," I said, forcing myself

to keep focused. "You want to use them to give the Librarian armies extra abilities."

She rolled her eyes.

"Don't try to claim otherwise," I said. "You want to keep the Talents for yourself; my father wants to give them to everyone. That's what you and he argued about, isn't it? When you discovered the way to collect the Sands of Rashid, you disagreed on how the Talents were to be used."

"You could say that," she said.

"My father wanted to bless people with them; you wanted to keep them for the Librarians."

"Yes," she said frankly.

I froze, blinking. I hadn't expected her to actually answer me on that. "Oh. Er. Well. Hmm." Maybe I should have paid more attention to the "ruthless, malevolent, egocentric Librarian bent on controlling the world" part of her description.

"Now that we're past the obvious part," Shasta said dryly, "shall we continue with our conversation about the Incarna?"

"All right," I said. "So what went wrong? Why are the Talents so hard to control?"

"We don't know for certain," she said. "The sources—the few I've had read to me with the Translator's Lenses—are contradictory. It seems that some *thing* became tied up in the Talents, some source of energy or power that the Incarna were using to change their soul vibrations. It tainted the Talents, made them work in a way that was more destructive and unpredictable."

The Dark Talent . . . I thought, again remembering those haunting words I'd read in the tomb of Alcatraz the First.

"You asked why I tell you this," Shasta said, studying me through the bars. "Well, you have proven very . . . persistent in interfering with my activities. Your presence here in Tuki Tuki means I cannot afford to discount you any longer. It is time for an alliance."

I blinked in shock. "*Excuse* me?"

"An alliance. Between you and me, to serve the greater good."

"And by serving the greater good, you mean serving yourself."

She raised an eyebrow at me. "Don't tell me you haven't figured it out yet. I thought you were clever."

"Pretend I'm stoopiderifous instead," I said.

"What happened to the Incarna?"

"They fell," I said. "The culture was destroyed."

"By what?"

"We don't know. It must have been something incredible, something sweeping, something . . ."

And I got it. Finally. I should have seen it much earlier; you probably did. Well, you're smarter than I am.

I suspected something might be wrong during my father's speech in Nalhalla, when he announced that he wanted to give everyone a Talent. But I hadn't realized the full scope of it, the full danger.

"Something destroyed the Incarna," I found myself saying. "Something so fearsome that my ancestor Alcatraz the First broke his own language to keep anyone from repeating it . . ."

"It was this," Shasta said softly, intensely. "The secret of the Talents. Think of what it would be like. Every person with a Talent? The Smedry clan alone has a terrible reputation for destruction, accident, and insanity. Philosophers have guessed that the Talents—the wild nature of them, the unpredictability of your lives when you are young—is what makes you all so reckless."

"And if everyone had them . . ." I said. "It would be chaos. Everyone would be getting lost, multiplying bears, breaking things . . ."

"It destroyed the Incarna," Shasta said. "Attica refused to believe my warnings. He *insists* that the information must be given to all, that it's a 'Librarian' ideal to withhold it from the world. But sometimes, complete freedom of information isn't a good thing. What if every person on the planet had the ability, resources, and knowledge to make a nuclear weapon? Would that be a good thing? Sometimes, secrets are *important*."

I wasn't sure I agreed with that . . . but she made a compelling argument. I looked at her, and realized that she sounded—for once in her life—completely honest. She had her arms folded, and seemed distraught.

I suspected that she still loved my father. The Truthfinder's Lens had given me a hint of that months before. But she worked hard to stop him, to steal the Translator's Lenses, to keep the Sands of Rashid from him. Even going so far as to use her own son as a decoy and a trap to catch those sands.

Hesitantly, I pulled out the Truthfinder's Lens. She wasn't looking at me, but staring off into the distance. "This information is *too dangerous*," she said, and the words were true— at least, she believed they were.

"If I could stop anyone from getting the knowledge, I would," she continued. She seemed to have forgotten for the moment that I was there. "The book we found in Nal-halla? I burned it. Gone forever. But that's not going to stop Attica. He'll find a way unless I stop him somehow. Biblioden was right. This *must* be contained. For the good of everyone. For the good of my son. For the good of Attica himself . . ."

My Lens showed that it was all truth. I lowered it, and in a moment of terrible realization, I understood something. My mother wasn't the bad guy in all of this.

My father was.

Was it possible that the Librarians might actually be *right*?

Chapter
4815162342

Standing there in that abandoned zoo, I had a moment of understanding. A terrible one that was both awesome and awful, regardless of the definitions you use.

It was much like the moment I'd had when I first saw the map of the world hanging in that Library in my hometown. It had shown continents I didn't expect to see. Confronting it had forced my mind to expand, to reach, to stretch and grab hold of space it hadn't known about previously.

After spending so much time with Grandpa Smedry and the others, I had understandably come to see things as they did. The Smedry way was to be bold almost to the point of irresponsibility. We were an untamed bunch, meddling in important events, taking huge risks. We did a lot of good, but that was because we were carefully channeled by the Knights of Crystallia and our own sense of honor.

But what if *everyone* acted like that? My mother's analogy was a good one. If every person were given a bomb big enough to destroy a city, most would probably be responsible with it. But it took only one mistake to ruin everything.

Were the Librarians *right* to want to contain some information?

I thought they might have been. But, of course, they were wrong about a lot of other things. They controlled too much, and they sought to enforce their way by conquering people. They lied, they distorted, and they suppressed.

But it was still possible for them to be right on occasion, when members of my family were wrong. And it was *very* possible that my mother—arrogant, conniving, and dismissive as she was—was doing something noble, while my father was being reckless.

If he got what he wanted, it could destroy the world.

Standing there, thinking about it, everything changed. Or perhaps I changed and the world stayed the same. Or maybe we both changed.

Sometimes I wished that darn river of Heraclitus's would just *stay still*. So long as it wasn't moving, it was easy to figure it out, get a perspective on it.

But that's not how life is. And sometimes the people who used to be your enemies become your allies instead.

"I see that you understand," Shasta said.

"I do."

"Then do we have a truce?" she asked. "You and I will work together to stop him?"

"I have to think about it first."

"Don't take too long," she said, glancing upward. "Tuki Tuki is doomed. We'll need to get to the catacombs and do our business there quickly, then escape before the city falls."

"I'm *not* abandoning Tuki Tuki!" I snapped.

"There's no use fighting now," she said, pointing to the sky. "Not with that hole in the dome. The Order of the Shattered Lens has ro-bats. They'll be flying through there to drop on the city in moments."

"Wait," I said. "Ro-bats. Are those, by chance, giant robotic bats?"

"Of course."

"That's the most stoopiderific thing I've ever heard of."

"Oh, and what would you call them?"

"Woe-bots, of course," I said. "Since they bring woe and destruction. Duh."

She rolled her eyes. Too much eye rolling.

"Either way, I'm not going to leave. The Mokians are depending on me. They *need* me."

"Alcatraz," she said, folding her arms. "We are working for the preservation of *humankind itself.* Compared to that, one city is unimportant. Do you think it was easy for me to treat you like I did, all those years? It was because I knew that something more important was at stake!"

"Right," I said, walking away. "You should win an award for your downright *wonderful* mothering instincts, Shasta."

"Alcatraz!"

I kept walking. Too many things didn't make sense; I had to sort through them. As I walked, Aluki and Aydee Ecks ran up to me, he holding his flaming spear, she with her backpack full of bears on her shoulder.

"Your Majesty," Aluki said urgently. "Lady Aydee just brought us word. The scouts have spotted something outside the city. We're in trouble."

"Giant robotic bats?" I asked.

"Yes."

"How many?"

"Hundreds, Alcatraz!" Aydee said. "I started to do the math but Aluki stopped me. . . ."

"Probably for the best," I said.

"They must have been waiting until the dome broke open to surprise us," Aluki said. "Your Majesty, they'll be able to drop *thousands* of troops through that hole! We have no kind of air force. We'll be destroyed in minutes!"

"I . . ."

Aluki and Aydee looked at me, eyes urgent. Needful.

"I don't know what to do," I whispered, hand to my head.

"You have to know what to do," Aluki said. "You're *king*!"

"That doesn't mean I have all the answers!" I said. My mother's revelation had shocked me, unhinged me.

Change. A man can be confident one moment—and then, with one discovery, be shocked to the point that he's completely uncertain. If my mother was working for what was right, and my father was the one trying to destroy the world . . .

I'd *saved* him. If everything went horribly wrong, it would be *my* fault. What else had I been wrong about?

But could I trust what my mother had said?

She's right, I thought, with a growing feeling horror. The words she'd said when I watched her with the Truthfinder's Lens . . . the things my father had said . . . what I'd read . . . my own feelings and experiences with the Dark Talent. All of these things mixed and churned together in me, blended like some nefarious smoothie from a gym counter in Hades.

The Dark Talent, *my* Talent, wanted everyone to be like the Smedrys. Somehow, I knew that Alcatraz the First had contained it within our family, limiting its damage and power. He was the reason why if someone became a Smedry, they got a Talent—but once one became too distant from the direct family line, children stopped being born with Talents. You only got to be a Smedry if you were cousins to the main line that ran from my grandfather, to my father, to me.

It was contained, but my father wanted to let it out. In the face of that, I felt so insignificant. So flawed.

"Alcatraz . . ." Aydee said hopefully. "We need a plan."

"I don't *have* a plan!" I said, perhaps more loudly than I should have. "Leave me alone. I just . . . I need to think!"

I rushed away, my pack of bears over my shoulder, leaving them standing there stunned. Yes, it was a bitter and childish reaction. But keep in mind that I *was* a child. The Free Kingdomers treat people like they act, regardless of their age, but I was still a thirteen-year-old boy. It was easy to get overwhelmed. Particularly when you learned you may have accidentally doomed the entire world to destruction.

It sounds a little odd when you say it, doesn't it? A kid like me, destroying the world? It makes for a ridiculous image.

(How ridiculous? Well, I'd say about as ridiculous as the image of a bunch of Canadian Mounties sitting on the backs of lizards while throwing cheese at one another. But that's kind of a tangent. Besides, that part isn't even in this book.)

Everything was twisted on its head. I should have surrendered Tuki Tuki. I should have . . . I didn't know what I should have done. Stayed in the Hushlands, with my blankets pulled over my head, and never gone with Grandpa Smedry.

I'd probably have ended up shot for that, but at least I wouldn't have put the whole world in danger.

I looked up. Gigantic steel bats were flying through the night sky toward the hole in Tuki Tuki's dome. Each one carried some fifty Librarians on its back.

But what could I do about that?

I turned a corner, walking down a grassy path between two zoo buildings, out of Aluki's and Aydee's sight so that they couldn't stare at me with those disappointed eyes. Overhead, terrible screeches began to sound in the air.

At that moment, the ground shook beneath my feet. I looked around, anxious, worrying that the Librarians had found more robots to toss boulders at the city. However, I quickly realized that the entire city wasn't shaking, just the patch of ground *directly* beneath me.

A hole opened up under my feet. I yelped, tumbling down into a tunnel dug by another Librarian infiltration team.

They'd just happened to come up right where I was standing.

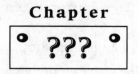

I'm afraid it's time to contradict myself. I know, this is very surprising. After all, I'm *never* inconsistent in these books. But it's time to make an exception. Just this once. Please forgive me.

Don't act this chapter out.

I know you've been following along since I told you to, acting out every single event in this book. When I saved the city by powering the dome, you were there, face pressed up against the window of your room. When I had my conversation with my mother, you were repeating the same words to your mother. (She was pretty confused, eh?) When Bastille and the crew were throwing teddy bears at robots, I presume that you ran through your house with stuffed bears, throwing them at anything that moved. And when I got out all of the boxes of macaroni and cheese in my house and mailed them to myself, you did the same thing, sending it all to me care of my publisher.

Oh. You didn't read that part? It happened between Chapters 24601 and 070706. Really, I promise. You should go act it out right now. I can wait.

Anyway, *do not* act out this chapter. You'll see why.

My fall ended abruptly as I crashed into a bunch of surprised Librarians. I struggled, cursing. Everything was jumbled together in the dark, dirty tunnel. There were limbs all over the place; it was like I'd fallen into a bin filled with mannequin arms.

Something looped around me, something made of wire and rope, and as I tried to scream out, something else got stuffed in my mouth.

About thirty seconds later, the group of Librarian soldiers slung me out of their hole, bound up in a net, a gag around my mouth. It had happened so quickly that I was still dazed.

The Librarians were wearing the standard bow ties and business suits—the men extraordinarily muscular, the women looking lean and dangerous—but their suits were camouflaged. They carried guns and moved with a sleek, threatening air. This was a particularly dangerous group of infiltrators—though, oddly, they didn't wear Warrior's Lenses.

I tried to scream out and give warning to Aluki and Aydee, who were waiting just around the corner. But the gag was firmly in place. The Librarians began to chat tersely with one another, speaking a language I didn't recognize. That surprised me, but it really shouldn't have. Not all Librarians in the Hushlands are from English-speaking countries.

I calmed myself, breathing in and out. My Talent would get me out of a stoopid net no problem. I just had to do it at the right time, when they weren't looking.

Several of the Librarians scouted around the sides of the alleyway, peeking out, while two others—a brutish man and a woman with red hair—knelt down and began to go through my things. The woman pulled off my pack, yanking it out through a hole in the net, while the man held my hands together and wrapped them with a tight string.

The woman pulled open the pack, rifling through it. She raised an eyebrow at the bears, but stuffed them back inside. Next she began searching through the pockets of my jacket.

That's when I got nervous. If they found my Lenses . . . It was time to escape. My Talent would probably surprise them, give me a chance to run. I took a deep breath through the gag and activated the Breaking Talent.

Nothing happened.

Well, okay. That was kind of a lie. Lots of things happened. Some birds flew by, a beetle crawled past, the grass converted carbon dioxide into sugar by means of the sun's energy. My heart beat (very quickly), the Librarians chatted (very quietly), and the Earth rotated (very unnoticeably).

I guess what I meant, then, is this: As far as my Talent was concerned, nothing happened.

It didn't engage. Nothing broke. I felt a moment of desperation and tried again. The Talent refused. It was like I could . . . feel it in there, seething, angry at me. Almost like it was *offended* by the things I'd talked about with my mother.

It had been a long time since I'd had trouble getting my Talent to do what I wanted it to. I had flashbacks to earlier years in my life, when it ran rampant, breaking everything I didn't want to but unable to break things I did want to.

I squirmed in my bindings, and the beefy Librarian pushed me down harder. He had a cruel, twisted face.

The woman said something, sounding surprised as she pulled my pair of Oculator's Lenses out of my pocket. I hadn't put them back on after using my Truthfinder's Lens on my mother.

The Librarians nearby all got dark expressions on their faces. The woman pulled something from her pocket—a kind of small gun. She pointed it at the Lenses in her hand.

They vaporized, turning to dust, then even that dust seemed to burn away. She shook the frames—which were intact—and inspected them, then tossed them aside.

That's right! I thought. *The Order of the Shattered Lens runs the army. They hate all kinds of glass.* That made me more frantic. I squirmed enough that the big guy holding me down grumbled and pulled something out of his pocket. Another type of gun.

My eyes opened wide, and I froze as he pointed it down and pulled the trigger.

And then I died.

No, really. I died. Dead, dead, dead.

What's that, you say? How could I be dead? I survived long enough to write this book, you claim?

Well . . . um . . . I *could* be writing it as a ghost. So there.

BOO!

Anyway, you're right. The gun didn't kill me. It fired some kind of dart into the ground next to me, attached to a rope. He fired another dart on the other side, and the rope tightened, holding the net—and therefore me—to the ground. The woman got out a knife and cut my jacket off of me.

That's right. My favorite green jacket, the one I'd been wearing since I'd left the Hushlands.

This, I thought with sudden fierceness, *means war!*

(And please don't tell Bastille that I was nearly as broken up about losing my jacket as I was when she got knocked unconscious.)

The two Librarians retreated, one carrying the remnants of my jacket. They left me squirming on the ground, pinned against the grass, gagged. I was desperate by this point. Up above, the flying bats were descending into the city, bearing Librarian soldiers. People screamed throughout the city, yelling, panic in their voices.

This is the point where I usually come up with some brilliant plan to save everyone. I tried hard, searching through my options. But nothing occurred to me. I was pinned down, my Talent refused to work, and I had no Lenses. About a billion Librarian soldiers were descending on Tuki Tuki, and dawn was still hours away.

Why is it I always ended up in these kinds of scrapes? My life over the past six months seemed to me like one bumbling disaster after another. I wasn't any good at fighting the Librarians, I was just good at getting kidnapped, locked up, knocked out, and covered in tar.

Just like my Talent, my wits failed me. It happens some-times, particularly when your victories seem so accidental, like mine often do. Besides, even if I could somehow escape the net, Tuki Tuki was still doomed. I couldn't stop thou-sands of Librarian soldiers.

It was hopeless.

To the side, the Librarians emptied my jacket pockets. They lifted up the Translator's Lenses.

And, with a flash, destroyed them.

My inheritance was gone. One of the most powerful sets of Lenses ever created, whose sands my father had searched for more than a decade to gather. And these Librarians had destroyed them without ever knowing what they meant.

Well, so be it.

Now, at this point, you're probably pretty frustrated with me. "Alcatraz," you're probably screaming, "you can do it, little guy!" Or maybe you're screaming "Hey, Bozo, stop being so depressed and *do* something!"

If you're yelling either of those things, might I remind you that you're talking to a book? It can't really respond to you. Do you talk to inanimate things often? (Man, you really are a weirdo.)

Anyway, whenever I'd been put in a situation like this before, I'd thought of some kind of brilliant plan at the last moment. However, it's really tough to be brilliant on command. Sometimes you get trapped, and there just *isn't* any way out.

I lay, pinned down, staring up at the sky. What had I really accomplished since I'd met my grandfather? I'd rescued my father, and in doing so had unwittingly helped him in his crazy quest to give everyone Smedry Talents. In Nalhalla, I'd gotten back my father's Translator's Lenses for him. Another step toward helping him destroy the world.

And now, here I was in Mokia. I'd accepted the *throne*, becoming king. For what? So I could convince them to keep on fighting when they should have surrendered? So I could make Bastille fall in combat?

The Librarians vaporized my Courier's Lenses next. Then they got out my Bestower's Lenses and my single Truthfinder's Lens. The Librarians vaporized one of the Bestower's Lenses.

There, I thought. *I've finally done it. I've failed.*

Above, in the air, Librarians dove into the city on the backs of their robotic bats.

And behind them, something appeared from the darkness.

Tiny at first, but growing larger. Shadowy vehicles flying through the night.

More Librarians, I thought. *That's obviously what that is. More Librarians, flying in gigantic glass birds. That makes perfect sense. My, those Librarians look awfully strange, wearing armor and carrying swords like that. One might even think that they're actually . . .*

I sat upright, shocked. Or, well, I *would* have sat upright, save for that whole pinned-to-the-ground-and-tied-up thing. So anyway, I lay pinned to the ground, tied up, but I did it feeling completely shocked.

There, swooping down out of the darkness, was a fleet of twenty glass vehicles with Knights of Crystallia riding on their backs. They dove behind the bats, dropping into the city. The sounds of yelling, fighting, and cheers of war rose in the air.

It had worked. My stoopid plan had worked.

Perhaps I should explain. Do you remember back right before Kaz ran off to attack the robots? You should—it was only like two chapters ago. (Too busy talking to books to pay attention to reading them, eh?) Anyway, I sent him with a message for my grandfather. "Tell him that we really, *really* need him here by midnight. If he doesn't arrive by then, we're doomed!"

You might have ignored the message. Of course we wanted my grandfather to arrive immediately; it was obvious.

But Kaz's explanation of Talents had changed my perception of them. The way we, as Smedrys, see the world, affects how the Talents work. Like Aydee—if she *thinks* there are thousands of teddy bears, then there are. Reality doesn't matter as much as the Smedry's view of reality.

Aydee's and Grandpa's Talents are very similar. She moves things through space and puts them where she thinks they should be. Grandpa moves things through time, putting them *when* he thinks they should be—so long as that *when* is a time he perceives as being late.

Does your brain hurt yet? 'Cuz if it does, try being me. Anyway, here's the short of it: You might think Grandpa's Talent works only when he's late. But that's not true. It works when he *thinks* he's late.

There was no way he was going to get the knights to Tuki Tuki on time. His Talent wouldn't let it happen. But if he *thought* that he was already late . . . If I could persuade him that he needed to be there at midnight . . .

Then he might just arrive at twelve thirty instead.

In the sky above, a bird flew by with a distinctive, white-haired man in a tuxedo riding on the back, waving a sword wildly like he was a conductor leading an orchestra. I smiled despite myself. I'd gotten my grandfather to arrive early—by tricking him into thinking he was late.

But I was still captured. None of the knights came near to where I was lying. The Librarians around me looked to the sky with shock, guns out. The one holding my Lenses—the

single remaining Bestower's Lens and my one Truthfinder's Lens—dropped them for the moment.

The fighting in the city grew louder.

This left me feeling very odd. I'd been convinced I couldn't save Tuki Tuki. But I *had* saved it. Or at least I'd taken a large step toward doing so. I hadn't failed them as king.

The *me* from the past had been clever enough to come up with a plan, even if the *me* from the future hadn't been able to. (Not *me* from the far future, that's the one writing these books, I mean the *me* from the slight future, the *me* tied up, which is actually the *me* from the past, as the *me* from right now is the one writing. Actually, that *me* is the past *me* too, by the time you read this. And actually—)

"Shut up!" I said to myself. Or at least I tried to. Being still gagged, it came out as "Shusmalgul pulup!"

There wasn't time to think about my failures, my past, or my future. Because my Librarian captors were focused on me again. One lowered a gun, pointing it at my head.

I felt a moment of panic. These were Librarians of the Shattered Lens. They were the most devoted, the most fanatical of all Librarians. And they hated Oculators passionately.

They knew what I was, and they weren't about to let me get rescued. The lead Librarian cocked his pistol. It didn't look like one of the fancy laser pistols used in the war. Just an old-fashioned Hushlander pistol, the kind that shot out a bullet and made you very, very dead.

I tried my Talent. Nothing. I struggled but was pinned tight. I could wiggle my right hand, but that was it.

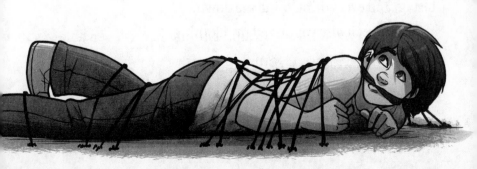

One of the Librarians said something, as if objecting to the murder of a tied-up kid.

The Librarian with the gun barked something back, quieting the opposition. He looked at me, eyes grim.

I panicked. I couldn't fail now! Not when everything was confused. I needed to *know*. Was my father right, or was my mother? What was this all about? I'd gotten the knights to Tuki Tuki. I couldn't die now! I couldn't! I—

The Librarians had dropped my pack right beside me.

I blinked, realizing for the first time that a small white square was peeking out through the open zipper. One of the pull-tag pins for the bears tucked inside; I could see a bit of purple fur peeking out behind the tag.

Frantic, I strained my fingers out and pulled the tag, yanking it. The backpack lurched up against me, but the tag pulled free.

The Librarian squeezed his trigger.

There was a *crack* in the air as the gun fired.

Something flashed in my eyes, the backpack exploding, vaporizing, the bullet vanishing in the air. The explosion washed over me, and—as I'd planned—it destroyed the net, the tag, and everything tying me down.

Of course, it *also* vaporized my clothing.

Now, perhaps, you can see why I asked you not to act out that last chapter. If you decided not to take my advice, then I really can't be blamed if you get in trouble for tying yourself to the ground, then running around naked for the rest of the afternoon.

Anyway, what just happened is something we call a teddy bear on the mantel. This is an ancient storytelling rule that says, "If there's an exploding teddy bear that can destroy people's clothing in a given book, that teddy bear *must* be used to destroy someone's clothing by the end of the book." Coincidentally, this is in fact the only time a book has included a teddy bear that can destroy people's clothing, and hence is the first, last, and only application of this literary law.

The blast radius of the bear grenade wasn't large enough to hit the Librarians. (Pity.) However, it was just large enough to vaporize the ends of their guns. It also dropped me into a crater in the ground that was some five feet deep. I could see the Librarians standing above, dumbfounded by what had happened.

I felt a surge of adrenaline. Not because I was still in danger, but because I was now lying stark naked in the middle of a war zone. And though the weather was tropical, the night air still felt rather chilly on my skin.

I'm SO glad I was unconscious for this —Bastille

I scrambled free of the hole, blushing furiously, and dashed past the Librarians. I stopped only long enough to scoop up my jacket—with the Bestower's Lens and the Truthfinder's Lens lying on top of it.

The Librarians finally began shouting and giving chase. The explosion had shocked them, but a naked Smedry seemed to have shocked them even further. I tried holding my jacket down to obscure the most delicate parts of my anatomy, but that made it really awkward to run. Keeping my skin intact was more important than keeping it covered, and I started

running through the zoo as quickly as I could, holding the jacket and Lenses in my right hand.

So it was that I tore around a corner, completely in the buff, and ran smack dab into the middle of Aluki, Aydee, twenty Mokian soldiers of both genders, and Draulin, Bastille's mother.

It was not my finest moment.

"Librarian commando superspy assassins!" I cried out, hiding behind Draulin, who wore her full Crystin plate armor and helm. "Following me! Gak!"

The group turned to look in the direction I'd come from. No Librarians followed. We all waited for a few tense moments, then finally Draulin looked back at me. "Er, Lord Smedry? Are you all right?"

"Do I *look* all right?" I asked.

"No, you look naked," Aydee said.

"Gak!" I said, quickly covering myself with my jacket, tying the sleeves around my waist. It had been cut off of me, though, so it didn't stay on real well.

"Ah," Aluki said, nodding. "I know this story. His Majesty is pretending to wear invisible clothing to show how stoopid we all are."

"I don't think that's how the story goes," Draulin said, eyeing me appraisingly, "nor do I believe that Lord Smedry is taking part in such an elaborate scheme. Those are grenade powder marks on his arms."

I looked down, noticing that the explosion had dusted my arms with a bit of burned gunpowder. "Er, yes," I said, holding the jacket in place. "And I *was* being chased by Librarians."

"It is well that we arrived, then," Draulin said. "Come with me, Lord Smedry. Aluki, you should take your soldiers and warn the perimeter guard that a group of Librarian infiltrators are haunting the zoo. They likely saw us up here and decided not to confront us directly."

The Mokian saluted, taking his soldiers and rushing away. Draulin steered me and Aydee toward a field behind us where a glass bird was waiting, this one shaped like an owl. I hurried forward eagerly, hoping to find some kind of clothing inside. We found Kaz waiting for us, a big grin on his face.

I hurried up to him. "Kaz! You did it! You got the message to your father!"

He shrugged modestly. "I should have realized why you chose the words you did, kid. The moment I spoke them to him, the ships all seemed to *speed up*, instantly." He eyed me. "You may have just revolutionized the way we think of Talents. If my pop's Talent can be tricked into making him *early* . . . Well, it will change everything."

"It's what we were already doing with Aydee," I said as Draulin and Aydee herself climbed into the glass ship. We stood in a kind of cargo bay at the base of the owl. "She's the one who sparked the idea in my head, actually."

The girl smiled pleasantly at that, though she obviously had no idea what I was talking about. It was her ability to keep getting fooled that made her Talent work.

Though . . . as Draulin sent Aydee off to the head of the owl to help pilot, I thought I saw a twinkle of understanding in the girl's eyes. Could she understand? Did she *know* *exactly* what was happening when we tricked her into adding things wrong? Sometimes living with a Smedry Talent requires a person to develop in very odd ways. As a child, I'd learned that everyone would hate me for breaking things and had compensated by pushing people away.

Could Aydee have learned to trick herself into ignoring numbers and speaking randomly, off the top of her head, when asked to add something?

Perhaps I was reading too much into that simple glance. I didn't really *know* what she was thinking, all those years ago. Here, wait a second. I'll go talk to her.

. . .

Okay, I asked her and she says yup, that's *exactly* what she does. Also, she said, "If you're writing about the fall of Tuki Tuki, you'd better make certain to include that part where we caught you frolicking in the zoo naked. I think you were seriously going crazy there, cousin."

Ahem. Let it be known that I was *not* frolicking. And the

naked part ended the moment a Mokian woman in the glass owl brought me one of those colorful islander wraps they wear, and I tied it on. There is NO MORE NUDITY. You can proceed with acting out the rest of this, if you want.

I stood on my head while singing "The Star-Spangled Banner" and juggling seventeen live trout with my feet.

Oh, wait. I hope you weren't wearing only a Mokian wrap like me. Sorry about that.

Aluki rushed up the gangplank a moment later, holding his spear. "The Librarians have liberated the captives in the zoo and the university! That's what they must have gone to do after letting you go, Your Majesty."

"Shattering Glass!" I said. My mother was free now. Her captivity hadn't lasted long.

And I *still* didn't know what I believed and what I didn't. However, as I looked out of the cargo bay of *Owlport*, I saw several Librarians fly their mechanical bats right into the walls of the glass dome. It shattered finally, falling in. The larger forces of Librarians outside the city surged into Tuki Tuki.

The city was burning. Huts aflame. People fought and warred in the night. Screams rang in the air. Shadowy groups moved against one another, struggling. In the background, an enormous force of Librarians—with hulking battle robots and wicked rifles—marched in through the open gap.

At that moment, I understood what it was to be in the middle of a war. And I came to a horrifying revelation.

The Knights of Crystallia were no cavalry come to rescue. Two hundred people, no matter how skilled, could not turn the tide of this war.

Tuki Tuki was going to fall anyway.

"Let us be going," Draulin said, waving to a Mokian who was in contact with the flight deck.

"Going?" Kaz said as the gangplank was raised.

"To Nalhalla," Draulin said, folding her armored arms. "We came here to get Alcatraz, after all. Now we can go back."

"What? No!" Kaz said. "We have to fight! That's why we brought you here, Draulin! Lower that gangplank!"

I simply stared out at the horrific scene.

Draulin stepped up beside me. "I'm not certain if I should curse you for forcing us into this nightmare," she said to me, "or if I should bless you for giving us the excuse to come and fight. Many of us wanted to, though we knew it was hopeless. To fight in one great battle against the Librarians, rather than suffering as they slice us apart kingdom by kingdom."

"Draulin?" Kaz said. "Blasted woman. You knights are all—"

"She's right," I said as the owl began to lift off. "I can see it. Even with the knights, Mokia can't win. If you'd thought you could make a difference, you would have come and helped, wouldn't you?"

"It was a difficult decision to make," Draulin said, and I could see that her eyes were solemn. Agonized. "It was the decision of a surgeon with two patients, one less wounded than the other. Do you abandon the more wounded, let them die while helping the one you can save? Or do you try to help the more wounded, and risk losing them both? We thought Tuki Tuki beyond help. Many of us still wanted to come and try anyway."

"So you're just giving up?" Kaz demanded.

"Of course not," Draulin said. "Now that we're here, we will fight. And die. But *my duty* is to get Alcatraz—and you other two—to safety. My brothers and sisters will fight."

And fail. The owl flew higher, and I could see just how big the Librarian army was.

I'd done it again. I'd thought I was saving Tuki Tuki, but I hadn't. Just like helping my father had been turned against me, I found my efforts here twisted on their heads. Not only would Tuki Tuki fall, but the majority of the Knights of Crystallia would be destroyed as well.

I'd accomplished nothing.

When I was young, trying not to break things had only

made it worse. Fix Joan and Roy dinner, but burn down their kitchen. Polish my foster father's car, but break it apart instead. It was all coming back to me, the times when the Talent dominated my life.

Things change. Perspectives change. The knights hadn't been cowards for refusing to help Tuki Tuki. They'd made a difficult decision, the right decision. But *I'd* forced them to come anyway, turning a huge disaster into a colossal one.

"We're just going to . . . leave them?" Kaz said.

"This ship has the king and queen on board," Draulin said. "There's a chance that we might be able to bring them out of their coma in Nalhalla." She didn't sound like she believed it was very likely. "You've accomplished what you wished. Now, at the very least, allow me to salvage something from the fall of this city."

My heart was a tempest of emotions, my mind a tempest of thoughts. I didn't know what to feel or think. How could everything have turned upside down so quickly? The arrival of the Knights of Crystallia was supposed to save things, not make it worse.

"What of my father!" Kaz said.

"Lord Smedry is leading the evacuation of the children and the wounded," Draulin said. "He will leave with them."

In the midst of my heart arguing with my mind arguing with my soul, one single thought pressed through the others. Something I could grab onto, something I could hold to, something *real*.

Bastille was still down there. And she needed me.

I ran through *Owlport*, leaving Draulin and Kaz behind. The ship rose high, sailing through the hole in the dome—the one atop the city, not the one at ground level. Glass rooms passed beneath my feet and to my sides, but most of these Nalhallan vehicles were constructed with the same general layout. I burst into the flight deck a moment later, Draulin and Kaz chasing behind me, calling out, sounding confused.

Aydee and a Nalhallan man I didn't recognize were in the piloting seats. "My name is Alcatraz Smedry," I said loudly, "and I'm taking command of this vessel."

The man blinked at me in shock, but Aydee just shrugged. "Okay, I guess."

"Fly us down there," I said, pointing at the Librarian army camp outside the city. I could see the place where they'd taken Bastille.

"Lord Smedry," Draulin said, disapproval in her voice. "What are you doing?"

"Saving your daughter."

Draulin showed a moment of indecision. "She'd want you safe; she is a knight and—"

"Tough," I said. "Aydee, take us down."

"All right . . ." Aydee said, steering *Owlport*. The vehicle wasn't terribly maneuverable—it was meant as a troop transport—and kind of lumbered through the air as Aydee flew it down toward the Librarian camp.

Most of the Librarians were invading Tuki Tuki, and the Librarian camp was relatively quiet. There were some guard posts and a couple of thousand Librarians as a reserve force. The prisoner tent was at the rear portion of the camp, and its flaps began to blow as *Owlport* flew down low.

A dozen or so guards raced out of the building. "Hey, Aydee," I said. "If we've got six plus six guards, how many is that?"

"Er . . . four?"

"Good enough," I said, and suddenly there were only four guards, the other eight having been sent away somewhere by Aydee's Talent. Hopefully they wouldn't cause too much trouble there. "Draulin, Kaz, four guards for you."

"Sounds good to me," Kaz said, Warrior's Lenses in place. He raised his pistols as *Owlport* settled down, face forward, resting on its belly.

Draulin gave me a suffering look, but opened a side door with steps down to the ground, and then followed Kaz out. They charged to engage the Librarian guards.

That was mostly a distraction. I took the other door out and slid down the wing. The floor of the camp was made up

of packed-down jungle leaves and fronds, trampled flat by
Librarian feet during the months of their siege. They rustled
as I ran around to the back of the tent and slipped in.

The Librarians had left their captives lying in rows. I found
Bastille near the center of the row, asleep in her tight white
shirt and uniform pants. There were several dozen others in
the tent, all Mokians. Officers or generals who the Librarians
had considered valuable as prisoners.

I felt horrible for leaving them behind, but there wasn't
much I could do. It was foolish of me to come even for Bastille, since we probably wouldn't be able to wake her up. But
with Tuki Tuki falling, with all of the mistakes I'd made, I
had to try to do *something*.

I slung Bastille over my shoulder and—teetering (she's
kind of heavy, but don't tell her I said that)—I jogged back
out the way I had come. Draulin was dusting off her hands,
Kaz holstering his pistols, the four Librarian guards unconscious on the ground before them.

And then a cannonball crashed through *Owlport*, smashing
in the side, blowing off one of the wings.

I stumbled to a halt. Another cannonball followed, smashing off the owl's feet and toppling the massive vehicle to its
side. I could hear Aydee crying out from within as it fell. A
Librarian cannon team had set up nearby. The reserve force
of Librarian soldiers were running out in front of it.

"No!" I cried.

Draulin shot me a withering gaze, something that said, "This is your fault, Smedry." Then she pulled out her sword and rushed at the Librarians. "Run!" she yelled at me. "Lose yourself in the forest!"

I just stood there. I couldn't carry Bastille with me, and I wouldn't leave her.

Draulin charged against an army of several hundred. That seemed a metaphor for everything that had gone wrong in this whole siege. But instead of making me feel sick or depressed like it had earlier, this just made me feel *angry*.

"Go away!" I screamed at the advancing Librarians. "Leave us alone!"

Something stirred inside of me, something that felt *immense*. Like an enormous serpent, shifting, moving, awakening.

"I want everything to make sense again!" I screamed. Saving Bastille had turned out like everything else. Draulin and Aydee would get captured because of me, and Bastille would remain in a coma.

I'd failed Bastille.

I'd failed the Mokians.

I'd failed the entirety of the Free Kingdoms.

It was too much. It seemed to well up inside of me. Rocks around me began to shatter, popping like popcorn. The tent behind me frayed, the woven threads that made up its fabric coming undone and falling apart.

There had been a time when I hadn't known how to control my Talent. When I hadn't *tried* to. I went back to that time.

Alcatraz the First had named the Breaking Talent the "Dark Talent." Well, sometimes darkness can serve us, work for us. It welled up inside me, bursting free, rising above me like an enormous and terrible cloud.

Reports of that day are conflicting. Some people say they could see the Talent take shape, like a giant snake with burning eyes, insubstantial and incorporeal. Others only felt the massive earthquake I caused, shaking the ground all around, opening enormous rifts around Tuki Tuki.

I didn't notice any of that. I felt I was in the middle of an intense storm, spinning around me like a cyclone. It tried to get free, tried to rip completely out of me, and I held to it, clinging, trying to force it back inside.

Reports say it lasted only for the length of two heartbeats. It felt like hours to me as I struggled, both terrified and in awe of the thing I'd let loose. With a heave of strength, I pulled it back into me. In a second it was contained.

I blinked, standing in the night. There were a dozen enormous cracks in the ground around me. The Librarians who had been running for me had been knocked down.

Unfortunately, the fighting in Tuki Tuki was still going on. I wasn't done. I took the thing inside of me and suddenly knew what to do with it. I reached down, pulling the single remaining Bestower's Lens from the pouch in my pocket. I knelt beside Bastille, who lay on the ground next to me. I brushed back her hair and exposed her Fleshstone. It was crystalline and pure, translucent, like an enormous diamond set into the skin of her neck.

That stone connected all of the Knights of Crystallia together. I raised the Bestower's Lens and looked into the Fleshstone, *willing* my Talent to pass into the stone.

It refused to move. It seethed within me, angry that I had stopped it from destroying. I gritted my teeth, furious, but I was feeling exhausted from all that had happened. I couldn't force it.

So I tried a different tactic. *I need to trick it*, I thought. Grandpa had to be tricked into thinking he was late so that he could arrive early. Aydee had to be confused by numbers so that she could add incorrectly.

What did I need to make my Talent work? *I need to think it's breaking something important*, I realized. Always, during my childhood, the Talent had acted to shatter, destroy, or break things that were very important to me or to those who cared for me. As I realized this, I found myself hating it again. But there was no time for that.

I focused on the Fleshstone, and I thought about how much I cared for Bastille. How important she'd become to me recently, and how if that stone broke, she'd die. The Talent—gleeful for something to destroy—snapped from me, but I raised the Bestower's Lens and channeled it, sending the Talent into Bastille's Fleshstone.

I felt an immediate *draining* within me as something very powerful was pulled through that Lens and sent into the stone on Bastille's neck.

It sapped me, sucked away what strength I had left. Everything went dark, and I collapsed.

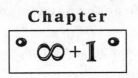

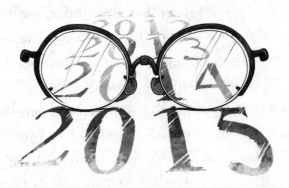

hree hours later, the sun rose over a broken city.

I sat up in my bed, looking out the window. Tuki Tuki was in shambles; many of the huts had collapsed. Broken spears, bits of metal, and shards of glass lay peppering the lawns of fallen homes. Pieces of trash blew in the wind.

There were no bodies, but I could see blood. The bodies had been removed.

"Ah, lad, you're awake."

I turned to find my grandfather sitting in the chair beside my bed. I was in the palace, one of the few buildings that hadn't fallen during the earthquake.

"What happened?" I asked softly, raising a hand to my head. It throbbed.

"You saved us," he said. He seemed . . . oddly subdued. For my grandfather, at least. "My, my, lad," he said. "That was something incredible you did! I'm . . . not sure what it was, but it was something incredible indeed!"

"What do you mean?" I asked.

"The Librarian weapons fell apart," Grandpa said. "In the middle of the battle. Every gun, grenade, cannon, robot, everything they had. It all just . . . well, lad, it *broke*."

I could hear drums. The Mokians were having a celebration. How could they celebrate when their city was in shambles?

Because they still have *a city*, I thought. *Broken though it is.*

"How are you feeling, lad?" Grandpa asked, scooting his chair closer to me.

"Fine, actually," I replied. "Tired. No, *exhausted*. But remarkably good."

"Well, that's great. Fantastic, in fact! Excellent to hear." He seemed hesitant about something. "I don't want to push, lad, but . . . do you mind me asking what you did?"

"Well," I said, "I knew that the Fleshstones on the necks of the Crystin are all connected. And once, when using the Bestower's Lenses you gave me, I lent someone else my Talent. So I figured . . . well, if I gave my Talent to all of the Knights

at once, while they were fighting, it would work for them like it did for me. It would destroy the weapons of the Librarians when they tried to fire."

My grandfather seemed disturbed. "Ah . . ." he said. "Yes, very clever, very clever."

"It wasn't supposed to be clever," I said, grimacing. "It just kind of . . . *happened*. But it looks like it worked."

"Oh, it worked all right," Grandpa said. "Maybe better than you thought . . ."

"What?" I asked.

"Well, lad, here's the thing. You didn't just break the weapons of the Librarians who were fighting here. You broke them all, every weapon being wielded by a Librarian *anywhere* in Mokia. In one moment they all shattered, broke, fell apart." Grandpa raised a hand to his head, scratching at the fluffy white hair there. "They've retreated, called off the war, and gone back to the Hushlands. The Mokians have named you a national hero."

I sat back, stunned.

"Already the news is spreading through the Free Kingdoms," Grandpa said. "This is the first time the Librarians have been turned away from taking a kingdom they were besieging. It's being called a miracle. You're a hero, lad. Everyone is talking about it."

"I . . ." I felt odd. I should have felt like celebrating, jumping up and screaming for joy. But I still felt troubled and worried. Something inside of me had changed. Being forced to confront my conceptions of what was right and what was wrong, who was good and who was evil, had changed me.

I didn't want to celebrate, I wanted to hide. The world was a scary place. My Talent terrified me suddenly, even after I'd used it to save so many.

"Lad," Grandpa said. "Do you know when the Talents . . . might come back?"

I felt a chill. "What do you mean?"

"None of them work anymore," Grandpa said. "Me, Kaz, Aydee . . . no more Talents. They're gone."

Hesitantly, I reached out and touched the bed frame, engaging my Talent. But nothing happened. It wasn't like before, when I felt reluctance within me. Now there was just a void, an emptiness where my Talent had once been.

I let it out, I thought. *It can't be! I contained it, kept it from destroying! I pulled it back in!*

But I'd done something else. I'd . . . well, somehow, I'd *broken the Smedry Talents.*

"I don't know," I said. "I don't know anything."

"Ah. Well, then, lad, you should rest. Rest indeed . . ."

* * *

When I next awoke, I had a stream of visitors. Aluki, Aydee, Kaz, then countless Mokians wishing to show their appreciation for me saving their city.

I tried to explain that I'd *destroyed* their city, but they weren't listening. The Librarians had retreated; Mokia was safe. What was left of it, at least.

I kept waiting to see if Bastille, the king, or the queen would come to see me. None of them did, though someone did bring me a cheese sandwich and insist that I eat it, thereby fulfilling the holy prophecy of the Foreword, as was spoken by Alcatraz Smedry.

Finally, I asked the question I'd been dreading and got the answer I'd feared. Those who'd been knocked unconscious during the war were still in comas. The Librarians had fled, taking the antidote with them.

Mokian scientists were confident they could find a cure, given enough time. But in the end, I had failed Bastille after all. And Mokia too—more than half of their population was still unconscious.

I didn't say this to the Mokians. Instead, I nodded and accepted thanks. I couldn't really explain how I felt. I wasn't the same person anymore. Too much had happened. Too much had changed.

I was finally free of the Talent, and that terrified me. Where was it? What had I done?

When I remembered that I'd lost my Translator's Lenses, that only made me feel sicker.

My final visitor of the day was a very unexpected one. She sauntered in, accompanied by my grandfather and two guards. Shasta Smedry, my mother. She still wore her Librarian business suit and skirt. Her blonde hair was down, and they'd taken her glasses as a precaution.

My mother could have been a pretty woman if she'd wanted to be. That had never seemed to matter to her.

"Lad," Grandpa said, "she insisted that we bring her to you. I'm not sure if it was a good idea."

"It's all right," I said, focusing on Shasta. "You should be gone. The Librarians who kidnapped me went back and freed all of you."

"Yes, they did," she said. "And I waited behind to get captured again."

I frowned.

"I think your father is going to come here," Shasta said, eyeing her guards with a raised eyebrow. "The catacombs of the Mokian Royal University are said to have walls that are inscribed with the Forgotten Tongue. I thought Attica would try to get to them before the city fell. Alcatraz the First was said to have spent much time in this area, so there's a high probability that the writings were his."

"Well, that's not an issue any longer," Grandpa Smedry said. "The Mokian university is no more. The entire thing was swallowed up in the earthquake, crushed flat, the catacombs pulverized."

"Is that so?" Shasta said flatly.

"Indeed," Grandpa said, meeting her stare. There didn't seem to be much affection between them. Of course, they were in-laws, so what did you expect?

"Where will he go next?" I asked.

Shasta turned to me. She drew her lips to a line.

"I'll go with you," I found myself saying.

"What!" Grandpa said. "Trembling Taylers, lad! What are you talking about?"

"We need to find my father," I said firmly. "I think he's going to try something stoopid. Something very, very stoopid."

"But—"

"You," I said to Shasta, "me, and my grandfather. Just the three of us, and anyone else you approve. You have my word."

She seemed amused at that. "Very well. There are rumors of an enclave of Forgotten Language texts in the heart of Librarian power. I suspect we'll find your father there. The place is carefully guarded, however, and even one such as I will have difficulty sneaking in."

"Lad, I don't know about this," Grandpa said.

"The heart of Librarian power?" I asked, ignoring him. "Where is that?"

"They call it the Library of Congress," Shasta said. "But it's really something far grander. The Highbrary, a bunker the size of a city, hidden underneath Washington, DC, in the United States, deep within the Hushlands."

That got my grandfather's attention. "The *Highbrary*?" he asked. He got an almost dreamy look in his eyes. "My, my. I've *always* wanted to infiltrate that place. . . ."

That's my grandfather for you. He might have lost his Talent, but he was still a Smedry.

"The Highbrary will contain the formula for all Librarian weapon antidotes," Shasta said, almost teasingly. "If you want to cure your friends, it is the place to go."

Grandpa looked even more eager, but he held himself back. "The lad and I will discuss it, Shasta. If we agree to this little endeavor, then you'll be coming as a prisoner, carefully watched over. That's the only way I'd agree to it."

Shasta smiled again, glancing at me. "Very well," she said, then waved to her guards—as if they were attendants—and had them lead her from the room.

My grandfather looked shaken. He sat down on the stool beside my bed again. "That woman . . ."

"We need to go with her," I said. "My father can't be allowed to try to give everyone Smedry Talents. Grandpa, I think that the *Talents* might be what destroyed the Incarna! I think—"

"Yes," Grandpa said. "Yes, you're probably right."

"What? You know already?"

"I've guessed it, lad," Grandpa said. "And feared it, after you told me what you found in the tomb of Alcatraz the First."

"Do you think my father can really do it?" I asked.

"If it were anyone else," Grandpa said, "I'd say no. But your father . . . well, he's a special man, capable of extraordinary things. Yes, I think he might just be able to do it, if he wants to."

"He's got the only remaining pair of Translator's Lenses," I said. "Mine were destroyed."

"Ah. I wondered why we didn't find them on you."

"He's going to the Highbrary. You know what we have to do, Grandfather."

He looked at me, then nodded. "Yes. But let's at least sleep on it a day and then decide."

I nodded back to him and he stood, withdrawing, leaving me to listen to the sounds of the Mokian drums outside. They'd celebrate all day, as per their tradition.

And then, on the morrow, they'd mourn for those who were dead. Celebrations first, sorrows second.

I didn't have time for either one. Mokia had been a diversion, a distraction, for both me and my mother. My father, Attica Smedry, had a huge head start, and what he was planning could destroy us all.

The Dark Talent was free, and the entire Smedry clan had lost their powers. An enormous fleet of Librarian soldiers was returning to the Hushlands with tales of what the Talents could do.

I think this is a good place to end, don't you?

Author's Afterword

Now you know the truth of why I'm lauded as a hero.

Sure, the things I did in previous volumes of my autobiography helped my reputation. But *this* was the event that everyone still talks about, the liberation of Mokia, the single-handed defeat of dozens of Librarian armies scattered throughout the Free Kingdoms.

My reputation was secure. I'd go down in history as one of the most influential people to ever live, and I'd be remembered as one of the greatest Mokian kings of all time. (If one of the shortest to rule—I was able to give up the throne to Princess Kamali the next day, when she came back to take over for me.) Sure, Bastille was in trouble—but you know that everything turns out all right with her in the end. After all, I've mentioned several times that she's often standing here in our house, reading over my shoulder as I write these things. All in all, I saved the day, defeated the Librarian armies, and permanently turned the tide of the war.

The funny thing is, in doing all these marvelous things, I'd changed into a completely different person. Your hero is no longer with us. The very act of heroism changed him. I'd walked into Mokia as one person, and I walked out of it as a vastly different one. That's nothing surprising; all people change.

Some changes happen slowly, like a rock being weathered away by the rain. Others happen quickly, suddenly. An earthquake shakes a city. A heart stops beating. A discovery is made, and a lightbulb turns on for the first time.

The Librarians . . . they try to keep us from changing. They want everything to remain the same inside the Hushlands. You remember when I talked about how they make all cars and planes look the same? Well, they do that with everything.

In this case, it's not because they're oppressive. It's because they're afraid. Change frightens them. It's unknown, uncertain, like Smedrys and magic. They want everyone to assume that things *can't* change.

But they can. I did. Alcatraz the hero was no more. If he ever was a hero in the first place. You've seen that most of what I accomplished happened by accident, luck, and a few random ideas that turned out to work. But even if you thought that sort of thing made him a hero, you need to realize that the person you worship is gone.

These four books are the parts everyone knows about. But the last volume, that's the part nobody understands. Nobody thinks to ask, "What happened to him *after* he saved us from the Librarians?"

I'll show you. Finally, you'll see. It will be amazing, eye-opening, awful, awesome, stoopiderific, stoopidalicious, stoop-iderlifluous, stoopidanated, and crapaflapnasti all at the same time. It involves an altar. Yes, that really did happen. I didn't just make it up. That scene with the altar is one of the most important events in my life. It happens in the next book, I prom-ise, no lies this time.

Maybe someday I'll actually write that book.

"I will not read the last page of novels first," I said, and then punched myself in the face.

"I promise, I'll never again read the last page of novels first," I said, then smacked myself on the head with a book.

"I really, really, *really* regret reading the last page of this novel first!" I said, then let my sibling, cousin, or best friend (take your pick) give me a wedgie.

(This page is, of course, here for those of you who skip to the end of the book and read it first. Naughty, naughty! Fortunately, you're acting out the book like you're supposed to, right? Well, let that be a lesson to you.)

The end.

Ah yes, the enchanted giant ninja squid-wombat that we never fought

—Bastille

ABOUT THE AUTHOR

When Brandon Sanderson's parents found their child talking to himself and pretending that all his imaginary friends were real, they were initially very concerned. They took him to a psychologist, who told them they had two choices—either lock him away for being completely bonkers or turn him into a novelist. Fortunately they chose the latter, and now it's perfectly all right for him to talk to himself and pretend that his imaginary friends are real because that's just the sort of strange stuff that authors do.

An afflicted man, he also has a terminal case of chronic smart-aleckiness, seasonal sarcasm disorder, multiple puns disability, and a mild case of the groaners. (Unfortunately, this tends to spread and give everyone else a big case of the groaners.)

Alcatraz sometimes wonders if it was a mistake to put Brandon's name on these books.

ABOUT THE ILLUSTRATOR

Free Kingdoms agents have confirmed that Hayley Lazo is not a Librarian spy. Her artistic representations of events in Alcatraz's life are so ludicrous that no one would possibly believe them to be true, thus preserving the illusion that these are simply fantasy novels.

ACKNOWLEDGMENTS

For help with these books, I proclaim the following people honorary Bazooka Bunnies:

The Indefinable Peter Ahlstrom, for whom the book is dedicated. He's believed in me longer than anyone else on the list. Without his help, my books would be a lot worse.

Emily Sanderson, who (despite my various lunacies) still loves me, puts up with me, and even married me.

Karen Ahlstrom, who gives great advice, and who also puts up with Peter reading her my books for date night.

Janci Patterson, who tells me what I need to hear about my writing. Bastille may be based on her just a tad, but don't tell her, because she might end up chasing me around with a sword.

Kristina Kugler, who taught her two-year-old daughter to put her fingers up to her mouth and wiggle them when someone asks "What does Cthulhu say?" (Does she need a better reason than that for an acknowledgment? Well, okay, she read the book too and gave lots of great feedback.)

• Acknowledgments •

Joshua Bilmes and Eddie Schneider, who fight for these books. They're our own personal Knights of Crystallia.

Jen Rees, who provided a sharp red pencil to fight off the goblins of bad writing.

Susan Chang, who champions this series for Starscape. Ingrid Powell for proofreading, Karl Gold and Megan Kiddoo for spearheading production, and Heather Saunders and Nicola Ferguson for the interior design.

Hayley Lazo and Scott Brundage for the fantastic illustrations, and Isaac Stewart for the map, art direction, and cover design.

Thank you all!

Turn the page for an excerpt
from Alcatraz's next adventure

THE
DARK
TALENT

Available September 2016

Chapter
Doug

So there I was, standing in my chambers on the day before the world ended, facing my greatest adversary to date.

The royal wardrobe coordinator.

Janie was a perky Nalhallan woman wearing trendy Free Kingdomer clothing. Technically you could describe her outfit as a tunic—but it was only similar to a tunic in the same way that a high-end sports car is similar to a broken-down pickup. It was more like a dress with a belt at the waist, and had a large bow on one side with stylish embroidery up the sleeves.

It looked nice, making it a complete contrast to the monstrosity she held up for me to wear.

"That," I said, "is a *clown costume.*"

"What?" Janie said. "Of course it isn't."

"It's a white jumpsuit," I said, "with fluffy pink bobs over the buttons!"

"White for the purity of the throne, Your Former Highness," Janie said, "and pink to indicate your magnanimous decision to step down peacefully."

"It has oversized floppy shoes."

"A representation of your magnificent footprint upon the kingdom, Your Former Highness."

"And the fake flower to squirt water?"

"So that you may shower all who approach you with symbolic waters of life."

I raised a skeptical eyebrow at her and walked over to the bed, picking up the poofy rainbow clown wig she'd brought for me to wear.

"Obviously," Janie said, "that is a representation of the varieties of cultures and peoples you served during your kingship." She smiled.

"Let me guess," I said, tossing the wig onto the bed. "The Librarians took this 'regal' costume worn by retired Mokian kings and, in my lands, gave it to clowns. That turned it into something ridiculous in the Hushlands, like how they named prisons after famous Free Kingdomers."

"Uh, yeah," Janie said. "Sure . . . Uh, that's . . . exactly what happened."

I frowned at her evasiveness. At the moment, I wore only a

bathrobe. My old clothing—green jacket, T-shirt, jeans—was gone. My jacket had been cut up, and the rest of my clothing had been vaporized in a rather unfortunate incident containing far too much Alcatraz nudity.

Outside my room, Tuki Tuki—capital city of Mokia—was utterly silent. The drums of celebration had stopped, as had the songs of joy. Their day of celebration past, the Mokians now mourned in silence to highlight the voices among them that had been quieted.

If I was right, that silence was about to get a *lot* worse. I refer you to the footnote* for proof.

"What else do you have?" I asked Janie.

"Well, let's see," she said, obviously disappointed I wouldn't wear the clown outfit. I might be a former king of Mokia—though I'd only served for one day—but if that was the traditional costume of my station, I'd go without.

She reached into her large trunk and pulled out what appeared to be a dog costume, with furred feet, a tail, and a headpiece with floppy ears.

"No," I said immediately.

"But it's the official outfit for a retired prince of—"

"No."

---

* People who use footnotes in books are very smart, and you can trust what they say.

Janie sighed, setting it on the bed and digging farther into her trunk.

"What is it with these 'traditional' outfits?" I said, poking the dog costume. "I mean, even without Librarian interference, you have to admit they're kind of . . ."

"Regal?"

"Ridiculous," I said. "It's almost like you *want* your former kings to look silly."

Janie shifted. "Uh . . . why would we want to do that? It's not like we want people to see former monarchs as foolish, so a ruler who has stepped down can never change his mind, stage a coup, and seize back the kingdom." She forced out a laugh.

"You're a terrible liar."

"Thank you! How about this nice cat costume? It represents the way you gracefully maneuvered the politics of the throne!"

"No animal costumes at all, please."

She sighed, then continued digging in her trunk. A moment later she cursed under her breath. The lights at the sides of the trunk had stopped working.

Curious, I walked over. Why did she even *need* lights? I soon saw that the inside of the trunk was much larger than the outside would indicate. The trunk was a neat trick, but nothing I hadn't seen before—in the Free Kingdoms, people use different varieties of glass to accomplish some pretty amazing things.*

The lights at the side were made of a special kind of glass to provide illumination—and that glass was powered by a special type of sand called brightsand. It worked somewhat like a battery for glass. (In the same way that shipwrecked people act like batteries for sharks.†)

Her brightsand for the lights appeared to have lost its charge. Fortunately, I knew something else that worked as a battery for both sand *and* sharks: me.

I reached out and touched the glass of her lights. I might have—somehow—broken the Smedry Talents, but I was still an Oculator. That meant I could power special types of glass.

I dredged up something inside me and pushed it out—it was a little like trying to throw up when not nauseous. The glass lights shining into Janie's trunk burst aglow, brilliant as the sun. I yelped, startled by the sudden explosion of power. Usually there was a sense of resistance when trying to do this, but today the energy came right out.

I stumbled back as the glass plates actually *melted*.

"Wow," Janie said. "Uh . . . you *really* hate these clothes, don't you?"

---

* Like adding footnotes to books.
† Footnote: It's true. Think about it.

"I . . ."

Let me pause here and explain an important point. When you are a coward like me, you should always take credit for something you didn't intend to do. You see, part of being a coward is being too afraid of not being seen as awesome to admit to not being awesome, though you have to be careful not to let on that you're too afraid of not being awesome to admit that not being awesome would indicate to those that want someone to be awesome that you are not as awesome as your awesomeness would otherwise indicate.

"I'm awesome," I said.

Sorry. I got a little confused in that last paragraph. Man, this writing can be as regal as a former Mokian monarch sometimes.

Janie looked at me.

"Ah, ahem," I said. "I saw a military uniform. What about that?"

I'd only seen a glimpse of it in the bright light: an outfit of Nalhallan design, with big epaulettes* on the shoulders and all kinds of ropes and ribbons and buttons and things, intended

---

* Epaulettes are those things soldiers wear on their shoulders to make them look more important. Nothing proclaims "look how macho I am" more than a good set of epaulettes. Other than, I guess, a big sign that reads "look how macho I am," but we wouldn't want to be *flagrant* about it, would we?

to make officers stand out on a battlefield and get shot first so the soldiers doing the real fighting are safe.

"I suppose," Janie said, "I can try to dig that out—but I'll need to install some new lights first." She glanced at the bubbling globs of glass on the sides of her trunk.

"Uh, thanks," I said.

"You *sure* you don't want a frog costume? Technically it's supposed to be for a retired king who served at least seven days, but you could swing it."

"No thanks." I hesitated, but was too curious not to ask. "Let me guess. The frog costume represents how a monarch leaps hurdle after hurdle as a leader?"

"Nah. It's symbolic of how you survived your kingship without croaking."

Of course.

Janie got out another pack and began digging around for some lights. Embarrassed at having ruined her glass, I made an excuse about needing to use the restroom and slipped out. In truth, I just wanted to be alone for a little while.

The hallway outside my room was decorated with a woven mat, the walls constructed of large reeds, the roof thatched. I didn't see a soul. The place was freakishly quiet, and I found myself tiptoeing. (A common action of cowards like me.)

It seemed to me that with everything that had happened in

the last few days, I should be doing something far more important than deciding what to wear. Tuki Tuki was safe, but I hadn't won this war. Not as long as Bastille and so many Mokians lay in comas, Librarians still ruled the Hushlands, and there were footnotes lying scattered around unused.*

We needed to chase down my father and stop him from putting his insane plan into motion. Though . . . maybe his plan wouldn't work anymore. I'd broken the Talents, after all. Maybe that would stop him from giving Talents to everyone else.

No, I thought. *This is my father.* He'd bested the undead Librarians of Alexandria and had uncovered the secret of the Sands of Rashid. He would be able to do this too. If we didn't stop him.

I heard voices in the hallway, so I followed them to a spacious room topped by lazy ceiling fans. Inside, my grandfather stood before a large wall of glowing glass that showed the faces of numerous people in a variety of ethnic costumes. I recognized them as the monarchs of the Free Kingdoms—I'd saved their lives at one point. Maybe two. I lose count.

Bald on top, my grandfather wore a bushy mustache and had an equally bushy ring of white hair that puffed out along the back of his head, like he'd been in an epic pillow fight and a

---

* There. That's better.

mass of stuffing had gotten stuck to his scalp. He was, as always, decked out in a stylish tuxedo.

"Now, I don't want to act ungrateful," my grandfather was saying to the monarchs, "but . . . Accountable Alatars, people! Don't you think you're a little late?"

"Mokia asked for aid," said Queen Kamiko, an Asian-looking woman in her fifties.

"Yes," agreed a man in a European-looking crown. I didn't know his name. "You wanted armies. We're sending them, along with the air guard, to help you Smedrys. What is the complaint?"

"My complaint?" Grandpa Smedry sputtered. "The war is over! My grandson won it!"

"Yes, well," said a dark-skinned monarch in a colorful hat. "Certainly there is still work to be done. Cleanup, reconstruction, that sort of thing."

"You cowards," I said, stepping into the room.

Trust me. I know how to spot cowards.

My grandfather looked toward me, as did the monarchs on the screen. The Free Kingdomers liked to claim that they are nothing like the Hushlanders, but things like this glass wall—which was Communicator's Glass, designed for speaking over long distances—are very similar to Hushlander technology. The two could be sides to the same coin.

The same went for those monarchs and the leaders of the Librarians. Politicians, it seemed, often shared more with one another than they did with the people they represented.

"Lad . . ." Grandpa Smedry said to me.

"I will speak to them," I said, stepping up beside him.

"But—" Grandpa said.

"I won't be shushed!"

"I wasn't going to shush you," Grandpa said. "I was going to point out that you're addressing the world's collected monarchs in a *bathrobe*."

Uh . . .

Right.

"It's a representation of my disdain for their callous disregard for Mokian lives!" I proclaimed, raising a hand with my finger pointed toward the sky.

Thanks, Janie.

"Young Smedry," said Kamiko, "we are grateful for what you have done, but you have no right to speak to us in such a way!"

"I have *every* right!" I snapped. "I am a former king of Mokia."

"You were king for *one day*," said a tiny dinosaur. I knew that one; Supremus Rex, monarch of the dinosaurs.

"One day is long enough to get some of the stench on me," I said, "but brief enough to not be overwhelmed by it. You send armies *now*? After the fight is won, and you realize that an alliance with the Librarians is impossible? I can't believe that you—"

"I don't have to listen to this," Kamiko interrupted, turning off her section of the glass. The others followed suit, switching off their screens until only one remained, a man with red hair and beard, looking sorrowful. Brig, the High King, Bastille's father.

I felt my anger fade, and I looked sheepishly at my grandfather. I'd stormed in and ruined his meeting.

"That was quite energetic!" Grandpa Smedry said. "I approve."

"I don't know," another voice said from the back of the room. My uncle Kaz was there, sitting and sipping a fruit drink, his adventuring hat on the table beside him. Four feet tall—and please don't call him a dwarf or a midget—Kaz was dressed in a leather jacket and sturdy hiking boots. He had a pair of Warrior's Lenses hanging from his pocket; he wasn't an Oculator, but he was pretty handy in a fight.

Kaz raised his cup toward me. "It was good calling them cowards, Al, but I think you could have slipped another insult or two in before they switched off their glass. And the send-off . . . yeah, that wasn't suitably theatrical at all."

"True, true," Grandpa said. "The dramatic effect of your intrusion *could* have been much greater, and you could have been far more annoying."

And that's probably the best introduction I could give you to my family. In the last six months of my life, I'd taunted undead Librarian ghosts, recklessly used my Talent to lay waste to armies, run headlong into danger a dozen times over, and aggravated some of the most powerful Librarians who have ever lived—but compared to the rest of the Smedry clan, I'm the *responsible, cool-headed* one.

"I doubt insulting the monarchs would do any good, Leavenworth," the High King said to my grandfather, speaking through his glowing pane of glass. "They *are* afraid. A few days ago, the world made sense to them—but now everything has changed."

"Because the Librarians were driven off?" I asked. Bastille's father looked very, very tired, with red eyes and drooping features.

"Yes," the king said to me. "Driven off by one person, and by a power they didn't know he had—a power they can't imagine or understand. They're afraid that what you have done will enrage the Librarians."

"Mokia was their sacrifice," Grandpa Smedry said, angry. "They foolishly hoped it would satiate the Librarians. And now they're convinced that the Librarians will return in force, determined this time to crush the entirety of the Free Kingdoms."

Politics.

I *hate* politics. When I'd first learned about the Free Kingdoms, I'd imagined how wonderful and amazing they'd be. I spent two entire books trying to get there, only to find that—despite their many wonders—the people in them were . . well, people.* Free Kingdomers had all the flaws of people in the Hushlands, except with sillier clothing.

I thought of Bastille, unconscious. She'd be so embarrassed to be seen that way. Those monarchs had abandoned her, and Mokia, for their own petty games. It made me angry. Angry at the monarchs, angry at the Librarians, angry at the *world*. I sneered, stepping forward, and slapped my hands against the Communicator's Glass on the wall.

"Lad?" Grandpa Smedry asked.

The glass beneath my fingers began to glow.

Perhaps I should have been wary, considering what I'd done to Janie's lights. I just wanted to *do* something. I powered the wall glass. I threw everything I had into those panels, causing them to shine brightly.

"You can't call them back," Kaz said, "not unless they allow you to—"

I pushed *something* into that glass, something powerful. I had certain advantages, being raised in the Hushlands. Everyone in the Free Kingdoms had expectations about what was and wasn't possible.

---

* I guess I was expecting marmosets?

I was too stupid to know what they knew, and I was too much a Smedry to let that bother me.

What I did next defies explanation. But since it's my job to try to convey difficult concepts to you, I'm going to try anyway. Imagine jumping off a high building into a sea of marshmallows, then reaching out with a million arms to touch the entire world, while realizing that every emotion you've ever had is connected to every other emotion, and they're really one big emotion, like an emotion-whale that you can't completely see because you're up too close to notice anything other than a little bit of leathery emotion-whale skin.

I let out a deep breath.

Wow.

In that moment, the squares of Communicator's Glass each winked back on. They showed the rooms of the monarchs, most of whom were still there, though they'd stood from their chairs to speak with their attendants. One had gotten a sandwich. Another was playing solitaire.*

They looked at me, and I somehow knew that my face had appeared on each of their panes of glass, large and dominating.

"I," I told them, "am going to the Highbrary."

---

* Yes, solitaire. What, you think kings and queens are *always* doing important stuff, like chopping off heads and invading neighboring kingdoms?

Is that my voice?

"You are worried I've started something dangerous," I said. "You're wrong. I'm not starting it, I'm *finishing* it. The Librarians have terrorized us for far too long. I intend to make certain *they* are the ones who are frightened and *they* are the ones, for once, who have to worry about what they're going to lose.

"Some of you are scared. Some of you are selfish. The rest of you are downright ignorant. Well, you're going to have to put those things aside, because you can't ignore what's coming. I know something the Librarians don't. The end is here. You can't stop this war from progressing. So it's time for you to stand up, stop whining, and either help or *get out of my way.*"

I let go of the glass. The images winked off, the wall turning dark.

"Now *that*," Kaz said from behind, "is how you end a conversation with style!"

Starscape Reading and Activity Guide to the Alcatraz vs. the Evil Librarians Series

By Brandon Sanderson

Ages 8–12; Grades 3–7

About This Guide

The questions and activities that follow are intended to enhance your reading of Brandon Sanderson's Alcatraz novels. The guide has been developed in alignment with the Common Core State Standards; however, please feel free to adapt this content to suit the needs and interests of your students or reading group participants.

About the Alcatraz Series

Brandon Sanderson turns readers' understanding of literary genres upside down and backward in this lively adventure series. In the world of thirteen-year-old Alcatraz Smedry, "Librarians," with their compulsions to organize and control information, are a source of evil, and "Talents" can include breaking things, arriving late, and getting lost. Add an unlikely teenage knight named Bastille, flying glass dragons, wild battles, references to philosophers and authors from Heraclitus to Terry Pratchett, and plenty of hilarious wordplay, and you have a series to please book lovers of all ages. And one that will have readers reflecting deeply about the nature of knowledge, truth, family, and trust, all while laughing out loud.

READING LITERATURE

Genre Study: Fantasy

In the introduction to the first book in the series, *Alcatraz vs. the Evil Librarians,* the narrator, Alcatraz Smedry, claims that his story is true, even though it will be shelved as "fantasy" in the world to which his readers (you) belong.

> **Fantasy** is a literary genre that often includes:
> - Characters who are magical, inspired by mythology, or who have special powers
> - Settings that include unexplored parts of the known world, or new and different worlds
> - Plot elements (actions) that cannot be explained in terms of historical or scientific information from our known world

While reading the books in this series, note when the author uses some of these elements of fantasy to tell his story. Students can track their observations in reading journals if desired, noting which elements of the fantasy genre are most often used by the author.

Older readers (grades 6 and 7) may also consider the way the author incorporates elements of the following genres into his novels, as well as how these genres relate to the fantasy components of the series:

> **Science fiction,** which deals with imaginative concepts such as futuristic settings and technologies, space and time travel, and parallel universes. Science fiction stories frequently explore the effects of specific scientific or technological discoveries on governments and societies.
>
> **Steampunk,** a subgenre of science fiction, which is often set in an alternative history or fantasy and features the use of steam as a primary power source. Steampunk features technologies which seem simultaneously futuristic and old-fashioned, or beings which are combinations of mechanical and biological elements.

After reading one or more of the Alcatraz books, invite students to reread the "Author's Foreword" to *Alcatraz vs. the Evil Librarians* and discuss why they think the author chose to begin the series by explaining where the books will be shelved in a library.

Technical Study: Structure and Literary Devices

The Alcatraz series can be viewed as the author's exploration of the idea, concept, and value of books themselves as both a way information is shared, and the way it is contained. One way Brandon Sanderson accomplishes this is to question the very structure of the novel. Invite students to look for the following elements in the stories and share their reactions to these literary devices and structures.

- Point of View. In this series, the point of view through which the reader sees the story is in the first-person voice of Alcatraz Smedry. He also claims that he is using the name Brandon Sanderson as a pseudonym, thus this is an autobiography or memoir. Is Alcatraz Smedry a *reliable* narrator, giving readers an unbiased report of the events of the story, or is Al an *unreliable* narrator, making false claims or telling the story in such a way as to leave doubts in the reader's mind? In what ways is Alcatraz reliable and/or unreliable? How might the series be different if Bastille or another character were telling the story? (Hint: For further examples of unreliable narrators in children's and teen fiction, read Jon Scieszka's *The True Story of the Three Little Pigs*, E. Nesbit's *The Story of the Treasure Seekers*, Justine Larbalestier's *Liar*, or Harper Lee's *To Kill a Mockingbird*.)
- Asides. At times, the narrator directly addresses the reader, suggesting how s/he should interpret a comment or how to best enjoy the novel (e.g. reading aloud or acting out scenes). Does this change the reader's sense of his or her relationship with the book? If so, how does this relationship feel different?
- Chapter Breaks. Discuss the unusual ways the author begins, ends, numbers, and sequences chapters. Is this pleasant or unpleasant?

Have readers read any other works of fiction (or nonfiction) that explore chapters in this way?

- <u>Wordplay in World-Building</u>. To explain *Free Kingdoms* ideas, technologies, and objects in terms of the *Hushlander* (readers') world, the author uses similes, metaphors, and analogies. To reflect protagonist Alcatraz's own confusion and frustration, Brandon Sanderson employs invented words, puns, and even text written backward or in other unusual ways. Find examples of these uses of wordplay in the text. How does the use of these literary devices enrich the text?

Character Study: Families and Friends

Having been raised in foster homes convinced that both of his parents were horrible people, Alcatraz Smedry is often uncertain as to what it means to like, love, and trust other people. Since he is the narrator of the series, Alcatraz's uncertainty affects readers' perceptions of the characters he describes. In a reading journal or in class discussion, have students analyze the physical traits, lineage (parents, relationships), motivations, and concerns of major characters in the novel. How is each character related to Alcatraz? What is especially important about the idea of family relationships in this series? Does Alcatraz's view of certain characters change in the course of single books? Do recurring characters develop or change over the course of more than one book in the series? If so, how and why do the characters evolve?

English Language Arts Common Core Reading Literature Standards
RL.3.3-6, 4.3-6, 5.3-6, 6.3-6, 7.3-6

THEMES AND MOTIFS: DISCUSSION TOPICS for the ALCATRAZ SERIES

Sanderson's Alcatraz novels can be read on many levels, including as adventure stories, as musings on the nature of knowledge, and as fantasies incorporating elements of science fiction and steampunk.

Here are some themes you may want to watch for and explore with your classmates or students.

- <u>Talent</u>. How does Sanderson use the word *talent* in traditional and nontraditional ways? Is talent important, valuable, even essential? What does Sanderson really mean by "talent"? How might students incorporate Sanderson's unique interpretation of the word talent into their own sense of self?
- <u>Heroism</u>. Throughout the novel, Alcatraz claims to be "bad," "a liar," "a coward," and "not a hero." What makes a "hero" in a novel, a movie, and in real life? Does it matter if a person acts heroically on purpose or by accident? What do you think is the most important reason Alcatraz denies his heroism?
- <u>Knowledge, Learning, Thinking</u>. Find instances in the stories when Alcatraz admits to acting before thinking ahead to consider all possible outcomes of his plans. In these instances, is he simply being careless or does he lack some important information since he was raised in the Hushlands? Compare and contrast the way people acquire knowledge in the Hushlands versus the Free Kingdoms.
- <u>Opposites</u>. Throughout the novels, the narrator refers to the ideas of the ancient Greek philosopher Heraclitus, whose doctrines included (1) universal flux (the idea that things are constantly changing) and (2) unity of opposites (the idea that opposites (objects, ideas) are necessary and balance each other). The philosopher also believed that "Much learning does not teach understanding," (*The Art and Thought of Heraclitus*, ed. Charles H. Kahn, Cambridge University Press, 1981). How might the series be read as an exploration of Heraclitus's doctrines?

English Language Arts Common Core Speaking and Listening Standards
SL.3.1, 4.1, 5.1, 6.1, 7.1
SL.3.3, 4.3, 5.3, 6.3, 7.3

RESEARCH AND WRITING PROJECTS

Keep a Reading Journal.

Use the journal to record:

- Favorite quotations, funny lines, exciting scenes (note page numbers).
- Situations in which the main character is in crisis or danger, and notes on what advice readers might offer.
- New vocabulary words and/or a list of invented words.
- Sketches inspired by the novels.
- Questions readers would like to ask the author or characters from the novels.

Explore Glass.

From Oculators' Lenses to unbreakable glass buildings, glass is a core substance throughout the series. Go to the library or online to learn more about glass. Create a PowerPoint or other multimedia presentation discussing the physical properties, history, practical, and creative uses of glass. Or create a presentation explaining how glass works in the Free Kingdoms. Include visual elements, such as photographs or drawings, in your presentation.

Silimatic Technology.

This part scientific, part magical technology powers much of the Free Kingdoms. Using details from the novels, create an outline or short pamphlet explaining the rules and functions of silimatic technology as you understand it. If desired, dress as you imagine a Free Kingdoms scientist might choose to dress and present your findings to classmates.

Choose a Talent.

Many of the characters in the Alcatraz series have talents that seem more like problems. Think of a personality or quality you consider a fault in your own life, such as messy penmanship, bad spelling, or the inability to catch a baseball. Imagine how that talent might prove useful in the world of Alcatraz. Write a 3–5 page scene in which you encounter Alcatraz and help him using your "talent."

English Language Arts Common Core Writing Standards
W.3.1-3, 4.1-3, 5.1-3, 6.1-3, 7.1-3
W3.7-8, 4.7-9, 5.7-9, 6.7-9, 7.7-9

DISCUSSION STARTERS AND WRITING PROMPTS FOR INDIVIDUAL TITLES

The Shattered Lens

The island of Mokia is under siege by the Librarians, and its fate may tip the scales for the Librarians' conquer of all the Free Kingdoms . . . unless Alcatraz can sort out family, enemies, friends, talents, and the power of exploding teddy bears.

QUOTES

Discuss the following quotations in terms of what they mean in terms of the novel; in terms of your thoughts about books and libraries; and in terms of their relevance to the real lives of readers.

Most members of my family, it should be noted, are some kind of professor, teacher, or researcher. It may seem odd to you that a bunch of dedicated miscreants like us are also a bunch of scholars. If you think that it means you haven't known enough professors in your time.

That's how they win. By making us give up. I've lived in Librarian lands. They don't win because they conquer, they win because they make people stop caring, stop wondering. They'll tire you out, then feed you lies until you start repeating them, if only because it's too hard to keep arguing.

Something stirred inside of me, something that felt immense. Like an enormous serpent, shifting, moving, awakening.

"I want everything to make sense again!" I screamed.

The Librarians . . . They try to keep us from changing. They want everything to remain the same inside the Hushlands. . . .

In this case, it's not because they're oppressive. It's because they're afraid. Change frightens them. It's unknown, uncertain, like Smedrys and magic. They want everyone to assume that things can't change.

WRITING EXERCISES

Reading Journal Entry: Who Is Right?

By the end of the fourth novel, Alcatraz believes that his mother, Shasta, is in the right while his father, Attica, is on a dangerous path. Write a journal entry describing how you think this new perspective will affect Al's relationships with his parents. Have you ever felt caught between two parents or other adults in your life? How might you use this experience to offer advice to Al about handling his situation?

Reading Journal Entry: Mokia

Imagine that you have arrived in Mokia along with Al. Write a journal entry describing the sights, sounds, smells, and emotions you experience those first moments on the island nation.

Explanatory Text: Hushlands vs. the Free Kingdoms

Imagine that you are a scholar from the Free Kingdoms assigned to instruct Alcatraz about the two worlds that coexist on Earth. Prepare a speech, including an introduction of yourself, your name, and your relationship to Al, then address the following questions: What are the key distinctions between these two worlds? How do characters move between the worlds? Can all characters do so? What do you think would happen to the Hushlands if they were made aware of the Free Kingdoms? Why are the Free Kingdoms so anxious to remain free from the Hushland society created by the Librarians?

Literary Analysis: Character Comparisons

Using information from the novel, create a chart comparing and contrasting the characters of Bastille and Draulin, Shasta and Attica Smedry, or another pair of characters of interest to you. Write a paragraph or essay describing the importance of including both of your chosen characters in the book. How does the contrast between the characters represent a larger conflict in the story?

Literary Analysis: An Alcatraz Handbook

From exploding teddy bears to myriad powerful lenses to terms like "stoopiderific," the Alcatraz novels have a vocabulary of their own. Create an Excel spreadsheet, graphic index, or other type of chart or booklet in which you list and define the language of the Alcatraz series.

Genre Exploration: Poems, Song Lyrics, and Beyond

In the course of the series, Alcatraz's talent is described as the most powerful, dangerous, and dark, yet he is a legend and a hero. With the complex descriptions in mind, write a poem, song lyrics, or a four-panel cartoon celebrating (or denouncing) Alcatraz Smedry.

English Language Arts Common Core Standards
RL.3.1-4, 4.1-4, 5.1-4, 6.1-4, 7.1-4
SL.3.3-4, 4.3-4, 5.3-4, 6.3-4, 7.3-4
W.3.1-3, 4.1-3, 5.1-3, 6.1-3, 7.1-3; W3.7-8, 4.7-9, 5.7-9, 6.7-9, 7.7-9

Read all the books in the Alcatraz vs. the Evil Librarians series!

Alcatraz vs. the Evil Librarians

The Scrivener's Bones

The Knights of Crystallia

The Shattered Lens

The Dark Talent